#2

On the Hockey Highway

THE MITCHELL BROTHERS SERIES

#2

On the Hockey Highway

THE MITCHELL BROTHERS SERIES

Brian McFarlane

Fenn Publishing Company Ltd.
Bolton, Canada

ON THE HOCKEY HIGHWAY
BOOK TWO IN THE MITCHELL BROTHERS SERIES
A Fenn Publishing Book

Copyright 2003 © Brian McFarlane

Fenn Publishing Company Ltd.
Bolton, Ontario, Canada

Distributed in Canada by H. B. Fenn and Company Ltd.
Bolton, Ontario, Canada, L7E 1W2
www.hbfenn.com

National Library of Canada Cataloguing in Publication

McFarlane, Brian, 1931-
      On the hockey highway / Brian McFarlane.

(Mitchell brother series; 2)
ISBN 1-55168-245-1

            I. Title. II. Series.

PS8575.F37O5 2003   jC813'.54   C2003-902102-5
PZ7

ON THE HOCKEY HIGHWAY

Brian McFarlane, with 53 books to his credit, is one of Canada's most prolific authors of hockey books. He comes by his writing honestly, for he is the son of Leslie McFarlane, a.k.a. Franklin W. Dixon, author of the first 21 books in the Hardy Boys series. With his father in mind and with two brothers not unlike the Hardy Boys as his central characters, Brian has created a new fiction series for young readers—the Mitchell Brothers.

NOTE FROM THE AUTHOR

In 1936, brothers Max and Marty Mitchell were living an ordinary teenage life in the North Country when a forest fire swept through the district, destroying everything in its path, including the Mitchell home and the newspaper office owned by their father. Max and Marty were at first accused of starting the devastating blaze after leaving a small campfire unattended. Not only were they forced to prove their innocence, but also they played heroic roles in the rescue of many residents of the town, including a close friend trapped in a burning hospital. What's more, the brothers solved the mystery of a bank robbery and helped capture the criminals responsible for the daring theft. Now, a few months later, the Mitchell family has been forced to uproot and move on—to another North Country community—the mill town of Indian River. There, new adventures awaited the Mitchell brothers; most of them centred around the sports they loved to play.

Brian McFarlane

CHAPTER 1

TWO NEWCOMERS IN TOWN

"I'll have a chocolate ice cream, please," Max Mitchell said to Brenda, the young waitress at Merry Mabel's Ice Cream Parlour. After school most of the kids attending Indian River High made their way to Merry Mabel's. Brenda was shy and tried not to blush as she scribbled on her pad, thinking that Max Mitchell had just rewarded her with the sweetest smile. And how many kids said please when they ordered? Max was the best-looking teenager in town and it was her good fortune to be able to take his order. Even if it was only for a five-cent ice cream. Her girlfriends would be so envious when she told them.

"And I'll have a banana split, Brenda," ordered Max's younger brother Marty. "Three kinds of ice cream, lots of whipped cream and three red cherries on top."

"Marty, that's going to cost you a quarter—half

your allowance," Max reminded his younger brother. "Cones are only five cents. And all that ice cream is going to add about six inches to your waistline."

"So? I'm bulking up for the hockey season," Marty explained, patting his stomach. "And I need a little fat down here to cover all those stomach muscles." He pulled up his shirt and showed his stomach to the other young men at the table. "Look! I've got muscles like Popeye. Did you guys ever see a stomach so flat?"

"That's not flat, that's flab," observed Kelly Jackson, bending to look from his corner of the booth. Laughter filled the air and more followed when Chubby Carlton, who had been sipping soda from a glass, belched loudly, causing heads to turn. Three teenage girls sitting in the next booth giggled when they overheard the mention of Popeye—a popular cartoon character in the 1930s—and Chubby's belch.

When the banana split arrived, Marty winked at the girls and said, "Want some?" They giggled some more and shook their heads no.

Marty and Chubby may have amused their classmates in the next booth, but when the girls turned their heads toward each other their hushed words were all about Max. "He's already won the starting quarterback position on the football team, replacing that know-it-all Barry Miller," Myrna O'Reilly whispered to her friend Lois Hull. "Max is the reason I decided to go out for cheerleader."

"And they say he's even better at hockey," Lois whispered back. "All that athletic ability and a top student, too. What do you think of Marty, his brother?"

Myrna shrugged. "Oh, Marty's all right. Kinda cute and funny, but he's much too young for us."

The Mitchell brothers were newcomers to Indian River. Recently, they had moved with their parents to the mill town after a raging forest fire, which was so common in many parts of the North Country in the 1930s, swept through thousands of acres of bushland, destroying several communities including their hometown of Haileybury. Max and Marty's parents, Harry and Amy Mitchell, owners of the newspaper in town, were forced to relocate. They settled on Indian River, 200 miles away, when the elderly owner of the *Indian River Review* decided to sell his newspaper to the Mitchells and move to Florida.

"What I want to know," Chubby Carlton said, covering his mouth to stifle another burp, "is whether or not you guys are going to enter the Big Race on Saturday. It's the biggest sports event of the year and you two should be in it. You're new in town and this will help you make some more friends."

The Mitchell brothers weren't fully aware of the

history and tradition of the Big Race, sponsored by the town's only industry, the Gray Paper Mill, employer to most of the residents of Indian River.

"Tell us more about the race, Chubby," Max said. "If we enter, we don't have much time to prepare."

"All the best runners in school will be there," said Chubby. "It's the first big athletic event of the summer. And some of the mill workers will be entered. The race is a tradition going back over 30 years—ever since the mill opened here in 1900."

"Will you be running, Chubby?" Max asked innocently. Hoots of laughter from the others in the booth greeted the question, but Chubby didn't bat an eye. He put both hands on his ample stomach and said, "You kidding me? I'm saving all my strength, and a lot of my weight, for the hockey season. Remember, I'm a goalie, not a marathoner."

"I'm a goalie too," Marty said. "Already we've got something in common, Chubby. And my brother Max is one of the best hockey players in the North Country. A scout from the Leafs wanted to sign him and bring him to Toronto last season. You know, to play junior hockey there."

"Never mind that," Max said, frowning at Marty. He was annoyed at his brother for talking too much. Marty was in the habit of telling people what a fine athlete Max was—especially at hockey—and it made Max uncomfortable. Soon after they had enrolled at

4

Indian River High, Max had made Marty promise not to tell their new friends about the brothers' adventures during the Haileybury fire: how they had rescued their friend Benjie from certain death in a burning hospital and how they had helped save Agnes Witherspoon, a classmate, from drowning. "And not a word about how we helped to capture those two bank robbers who chased us down the Shore Road. Nobody likes a braggart."

"I guess that's why kids around here don't like Barry Miller," Marty had responded. "He thinks he's the greatest thing since Babe Ruth. The guys were happy when you beat him out for starting quarterback."

Max finished his ice cream and turned toward his friends in the booth.

"Tell us more about the Big Race," he said. "It's just for fun, right Chubby?"

"Oh, yeah. But there's a 25-dollar prize and a nice little trophy for the winner. Barry Miller always wins. At least he has for the past three years. He's a fast runner and he knows it." Chubby pointed at his head then made a big circle with his hands.

"I get it," Marty said, "He's got a head as big as a watermelon."

"You got it," said Chubby, grinning. "Only bigger. And without a whole lot of seeds inside, if you know what I mean. Nobody can beat Barry. Just ask him.

But we'd like to see it happen. We'd like to see you two try."

Max huddled with his brother Marty. "Well, what do you think?"

"I think we should enter," Marty said enthusiastically. "I'm pretty fast but you're really fast. And five miles isn't too far. We're both in great shape from jogging to school everyday. Let's do it. If you win, you'll have enough money to buy me a new goalie stick for my birthday."

"Don't forget, Mom's birthday comes before yours. And she's a lot more special to me than you are," Max answered, half kidding.

Marty sighed. "Yeah, I guess you're right—as usual." He turned to the others in the booth. "Last summer we were playing baseball in the backyard. I dared Mom to try to hit one of Max's curve balls..."

Max chuckled and picked up the story, "I can't get over how she whacked that ball. High across the field and over the fence and all the way into Mr. Duncan's raspberry bushes."

"Yeah. And we got all scratched up looking for it," Marty said.

"I should have known she could hit," Max said. "Mom was a great all-round athlete when she was young. Dad says she was the best female hockey player in the North Country a few years back. He was a young reporter then and he covered a tournament she was in. That's how they met. That was the year her team—the Snowflakes—won the Lady Stanley Cup. Mom was leading scorer and tournament MVP."

"Mind you, we don't want you fellas to think Max is bragging about Mom," Marty said, giving his brother a meaningful look. "But it's all true." The boys in the booth were impressed. None of their mothers was the least bit interested in playing sports.

"My mom's an MVP," quipped Kelly Jackson. "Most Valuable Piemaker. Pumpkin's her specialty."

"It was Mr. Duncan who found the ball," Marty said, wanting to finish the story. "He popped up from the bushes holding the baseball over his head." Marty started to laugh at the memory. "His arms were all bleeding and then he took another look at the ball..."

Max interjected. "Just then Mr. Duncan saw that the ball was all wobbly, a seam had split and stuff was coming out of it..."

"And all this stringy stuff was falling on his bald head," Marty roared, cutting Max off. "Mr. Duncan looked like he had a white wig on. Then he yelled across the field at my mother..." Marty stopped, giggling like the girls in the next booth, ice cream all over his face. He rose from his seat, cupped a hand to his mouth and snorted loudly, catching the attention of every customer in Merry Mabel's.

Imitating Mr. Duncan, Marty shouted, "Why, Mrs.

Mitchell, I do believe you've knocked the stuffing out of this ball." Marty fell across the table laughing, forgetting the half-eaten banana split was now under his chest. Much of it now decorated the front of his sweater. He jumped from the booth, right into the path of a young man coming out of the men's room. The boys were laughing so hard they failed to notice it was Barry Miller. Miller was livid.

"I heard what you said, punk," he snarled, pushing Marty to the floor. "Head like a watermelon, huh?" He reached down to push Marty again. But Max shot from the booth, rose to his feet, gripped Barry by the arm and twisted it behind his back.

"Don't touch my brother," he warned. "Don't ever lay a finger on him."

"Let go of me!" Barry cried out. "Hey, that hurts."

Mabel shouted from behind the counter. "Break it up, you two. Or I'll take the broom to you."

Max released his grip on Barry who whined, "He started it." When Max pulled Marty to his feet, Barry pointed a finger at them. "Things were fine around here until you two came to town." He sneered. "You both think you're so hot." Chubby Carlton hid his head and snickered, while Kelly Jackson grabbed a menu off the table to hide the wide grin on his face.

"Think it's funny?" Barry fumed. "Well, I'll beat the snot out of you in the Big Race on Saturday—like always." He glared at the Mitchell brothers. "And that means all of you. If you're not afraid to run, that is." Barry turned toward the door, rubbing the arm Max had gripped. "Ah, why waste my time with a bunch of… a bunch of turtles. I dare you Mitchells to show up on Saturday."

When the door slammed behind him, the boys burst out laughing. Chubby howled and made turtle motions with his hands. Marty snorted up some ice cream and Chubby belched loudly.

Kelly pointed a finger at Max. "Barry's gonna make you eat his dust on Saturday. He said so. He's gonna humiliate you in front of everybody. I'll bet you're scared to run now."

Max grinned and said, "I'm terrified. I may have to hide in my room all day."

Behind the counter, Mabel winked at Brenda the waitress, then turned to the booth, shaking her head in mock anger. "You boys better finish up and get on home," she called out. "This is an ice cream parlour, not a comedy club—or a prize ring. And don't forget to leave Brenda a nice tip. Don't be like the birdies who go "Cheep! Cheep!" It's not easy serving a bunch of rowdy high-schoolers in a high-class establishment like this."

CHAPTER 2

THE FIVE-MILE RACE

"Holy mackerel!" roared Marty.

"What a crowd!" Max said, gripping his brother by the elbow. The Mitchell brothers were startled to see how many townspeople had shown up for the annual Indian River Mill Race on Saturday morning. "There must be a thousand spectators lining Main Street. That's about half the population of the town."

"And there are at least two dozen competitors," Marty said.

Max was a muscular youth with ash-blond hair and blue eyes. Almost seventeen years old, he was six-feet tall and weighed 180 pounds. He excelled at all sports. His brother Marty, two years younger and two inches shorter, had a thatch of reddish-brown hair and was known for his lively sense of humour.

Most of the race entrants were either high-school students or young men who worked in the mill. Marty nudged Max. "Look! Some of the mill workers are wearing work boots and overalls."

Their new high-school friends greeted the Mitchell brothers warmly. All, that is, but Barry Miller, the pre-race favourite. Marty overheard Miller say to one of his friends, "I'm surprised those two jokers showed up," nodding toward Max and Marty. "I'm gonna run them into the ground." Then he wandered off to warm up for the big event.

"What a sourpuss!" Marty said, jerking a thumb at Miller. Max shrugged. "He's afraid we're going to beat him."

"That's why we're here," said Max. "No sense entering a race unless you try to win it."

An older man holding a starter's pistol approached the runners. He was wearing a white jacket and sharply creased black pants. "Move up, men," he ordered. "Get up to the starting line. Race is going to start. Follow the arrows marking the route. And no cheating." A minute later he fired the pistol and the runners broke away whooping and hollering as they dashed down Main Street. Barry Miller took off like a gazelle, and soon opened a lead of 100 yards.

Max and Marty loped along in the middle of the pack, pacing themselves and breathing easily. There was still a long way to go. In the crowd their parents called out and the boys waved to them. "Hi, Mom! Hi, Dad!"

"You boys better pick up the pace," their father bellowed, his hands cupped to his mouth. "The Miller kid is almost out of sight already."

"He's right," Max said, lengthening his stride. He led Marty past several runners and soon they broke free from the pack. Far ahead was Barry Miller.

"You're faster, Max. Don't wait for me," said Marty. Max nodded and increased his speed, leaving his brother behind.

Soon Main Street was behind him and he turned onto the Mill Road, following the arrows, chasing Barry Miller. There were no spectators on this part of the tree-lined route. This was the road that discouraged most runners. It was unpaved, uphill and full of potholes. A recent rain had left the potholes full of water and Max had to be nimble to avoid getting his feet soaked. Even so, his shoes were soon caked with mud.

He started up a long rise and began to close the distance between himself and Miller. Through the trees, Max could see smoke rising from the stack at the mill and figured they'd soon have covered half the distance. Then it was downhill for several hundred yards and Max found himself moving closer to the fleet youth ahead of him. Barry didn't turn to look back. Apparently he thought he had no competition to worry about.

Arrows directed the runners onto the mill property

and because the mill was closed on Saturday, a lone watchman sat on a bench at the gate to wave the runners through. He was reading a Saturday Evening Post magazine. "Go right around the mill and come back out this gate," he told Barry. Then, when Max appeared, he repeated the instructions. "Seems like you two gazelles have left the other runners in your dust," he said to Max.

By then Barry had disappeared behind the huge main building of the mill and Max took off in pursuit. When Max rounded the corner of the building he almost stopped in his tracks. He was astonished. Barry had disappeared. He was nowhere in sight. *That's strange*, Max thought. *He wasn't that far ahead. How could I have lost him?*

Max passed a small open door swinging on its hinges. A bush hid the tiny opening almost completely from sight. If the hinges hadn't creaked in the wind, he would have missed it. Curious, he turned back. There were muddy footprints on the doorsill. He opened the door and saw a similar door on the far side of the building. A figure raced through the far door and slammed it shut behind him. It was Barry Miller. *He's cheating!* thought Max. *He took a shortcut through the mill.*

Max was outraged. For a moment, he considered cutting through the building as Barry had done. Then he put the thought aside and continued on.

He recalled some advice his father had once given him, "Cheaters never win and winners never cheat."

Max turned and followed the arrows that led him all around the building. He was now a good two minutes behind Barry Miller. He ran past the gateman who hollered, "What kept you? You get lost in there? The Miller kid was in and out like a flash. You'll never catch him now."

"Oh, yes I will," Max answered through gritted teeth. Far in the distance he could see Miller, running easily and confidently. Max burned to think of Barry holding the trophy high, accepting the cheers of the crowd and pocketing the prize money. *No wonder he wins every year*, Max thought.

Max increased his pace until he was almost sprinting. But he was wise enough to keep something in reserve. No sense catching Miller only to collapse from exhaustion with only a short distance to go. His long strides ate up the ground. His feet flew over the potholes. Coming in the opposite direction, led by Marty, came the other competitors, still jogging toward the mill.

"Catch him, Max," Marty shouted, "Miller's beginning to slow down."

The town was in sight now and soon the two race leaders would reach the end of Main Street. From there it was only about 400 yards to the finish line. Max pushed himself harder.

When Barry Miller reached Main Street he looked back and was stunned to see Max charging fast. The look of shock on Barry's face inspired Max to push himself even harder. Miller was gasping for breath. Max was now only 100 yards behind. The two runners turned up Main Street with Miller still in front. But he was struggling. His chest heaved and his legs wobbled. Max trailed by only 50 yards, but he too was beginning to feel the strain.

Forget your sore feet, Max coached himself. *Ignore the pain in your ribs! You can't let a cheater win this race.* Max focused on the finish line. *If I know Miller, he'll falter. He won't have what it takes to sprint all-out to the finish line.* Miller stumbled on, his head bobbing as he frequently looked back. His shoulders sagged and his eyes watered. He was trying desperately to summon enough willpower and energy to dash to the finish line and retain his title as the town's best runner. But Miller didn't have a finishing kick. He was all done. Finished.

The crowd was on its feet, cheering madly as the two runners approached the white tape. Only 20 yards left to go. Fifteen.

When Max reached Barry's shoulder, their bodies only inches apart, Miller glared at him and threw out an elbow. But Max was ready for anything from Miller and moved quickly aside. Miller desperately tried to snap the tape with a futile lunge that fell far short. As Max breezed past him, Miller stumbled and fell to the ground, sobbing in frustration. Max broke through the tape and fell into the arms of his friends. His dad rushed over and pounded him on the back.

"Great run, Max. Great run." He waved his camera. "I snapped a photo of you crossing the finish line for this week's *Review*." His mother gave him a big kiss. Several people, most of them strangers, came over to shake his hand and offer their congratulations.

Barry Miller did not offer any congratulations. He was not a gracious loser. Red in the face, he came over to Max and growled, "You tried to elbow me at the finish line. You knocked me down. I'm going to enter a protest."

Max almost laughed at the ridiculous charge. "I didn't elbow you, Barry," he said evenly. "You tried to elbow me. You can protest all you want and while you're at it why not mention how you ran part of the race indoors?"

Barry's face turned crimson. "What do you mean?" he stammered. "I don't know what you're talking about."

"Oh, yes you do," Max said. "I can show people the muddy footprints you left when you ran through the mill. You want to make a big deal of this, you'll be sorry. You want me to forget about it, I will. It's your choice."

Miller looked down at his muddy shoes. Then he looked Max in the eye.

"Okay. Forget about it, Mitchell." He walked away, his head down. Then he turned and said, "You may think you've won but you haven't. We'll meet again. You can bet on that."

Max saw a few of Barry's friends come up to him. Barry grabbed at his leg and appeared to limp. He complained loudly to his friends and his father that he'd run most of the way on a twisted ankle. He gasped in pain and limped off to have his ankle taped. His father, who taught math and coached sports at Indian River High, a man who stressed fair play and sportsmanship, watched him go. He turned to his wife and shook his head sadly. He said to her, "Barry just told me he doesn't want to live in Indian River anymore. Says he's not happy here. He wants to move to Chatsworth and live with my brother and his wife. He's angry and humiliated because Max Mitchell showed him up. Well, maybe it'll be good for him to get away for awhile."

Marty finished the race and captured third place easily. Marty congratulated Max and stood next to him beaming when Mr. Gray, owner of the mill, presented Max with a small gleaming trophy and an envelope containing the prize money. "Congratulations, young man. You ran a fine race," he said.

"Thank you, sir."

Mr. Gray made a short speech during which he mentioned the words "competition," "fitness" and "sportsmanship." It was obvious to the Mitchells that the residents of Indian River held him in high regard. He left in a chauffeur-driven limousine.

Marty admired the trophy Max had won. Then he wanted to see the prize money of 25 dollars. "Count it, Max. Make sure it's all there." Then he said, "That race was close. Barry Miller must be fast to finish almost even with you, brother."

Max smiled. "You might say he's sneaky fast, Marty. And he tried to elbow me at the finish line. He doesn't like me much because...well, I'll tell you later."

Marty said, "I think he's a sore loser. Look at him over there, whining to his friends about his sore ankle. Max, with your speed and stamina, I'll bet you could become an Olympic runner if you wanted to."

Max laughed. "Marty, there are hundreds of runners around who are faster than I am. Besides, I love team sports. That's why I'm beginning to like Indian River. There's baseball all summer and hockey all winter. Mom and Dad couldn't have found a better place for us to live."

"Let's go home, boys," suggested Mrs. Mitchell, putting an arm around each son. "There are butter tarts fresh from the oven just waiting to be devoured by a couple of hungry heroes."

CHAPTER 3

NO HELP FOR HOCKEY

The annual meeting of the Indian River Hockey Club held at the town hall was marked by a total absence of enthusiasm for the upcoming season. The club officers sat at a table sipping from coffee cups and talking about the weather. One man was working on a crossword puzzle and gave up when he couldn't think of a four-letter word for "Swiss Mountains." It had turned bitterly cold and there was a layer of ice on the river.

When Max and Marty Mitchell arrived, they climbed the hall stairs, made their way around a cleaning woman who was washing the floors and slipped into chairs at the back of the room. Their father, owner of the town's only newspaper, the *Review*, had predicted a dull session with no surprises. Over breakfast that morning, he had told his sons, "Tonight will mark the end of senior hockey in this community. It's unfortunate but there's nothing anyone can do about it."

Harry Mitchell had come straight to the meeting from his newspaper office. Notebook in hand, he was sitting with some friends in the front row. The story of hockey's demise in Indian River would be featured prominently in the *Review* on the following day.

"Indian River is a mill town, not like Haileybury where we lived before," Mr. Mitchell had told his boys across the breakfast table. "And Mr. Gray, the mill owner, is all powerful. With the economy in a slump and some bad actors giving a black eye to last year's team, I suspect old Harry Gray may not be keen to invest a thin dime in local sports teams anymore. And that's too bad for kids who love to play and fans who like to watch."

Max and Marty had found it hard to believe that any town in the North Country, especially a town with one of the biggest paper mills in the world, would drop its support for the local hockey team. Hockey had a huge following in big cities like Toronto, Chicago, Montreal, New York, Detroit and Boston—all members of the National Hockey League. Everyone was talking about a recent playoff game between the Detroit Red Wings and the Montreal Maroons, one that required a record-breaking six periods of overtime, before the Red Wings finally won 1-0. Unbeknownst to their parents, the

Mitchell brothers had listened to every minute of the game on the radio in their bedroom—until 2:30 a.m. They could barely stagger out of bed and get ready for school the next morning.

Max and Marty were convinced the sport had a bright future and often wondered if they would grow up and be a part of it. Everyone knew about the famous Stanley Cup and how fiercely teams had battled over it for decades—ever since Lord Stanley, Canada's Governor General, had donated it in 1893. They couldn't understand why a mill town in the North Country was attempting to abolish a game that almost every young person played and almost everybody enjoyed.

Inside the hall, the brothers soon learned why interest in hockey in Indian River was at an all-time low. "Who's the guy in the fancy duds and the slicked-back hair?" whispered Marty. "Looks like he bought that suit from Bozo the Clown." The hockey club president, a young man named Myron Seymour, wearing a pinstriped suit and spats over his polished shoes, stood up to address the small group in attendance. Marty's comment drew a frown of reproach from his older brother, but Marty continued to smile at his own little joke. Then he added, "Looks like he soaks his hair in crankcase oil."

"Hush, Marty, this is a serious meeting. That's Mr. Gray's public relations man," answered Max.

"Name's Myron Seymour."

"Geez, he's young looking for such a big job," observed Marty. "He must be related to the boss."

"Hush," said Max for the second time.

Seymour began to speak. "Gentlemen, I'm here tonight representing Mr. Gray, the chief executive officer of the Indian River Mill and it's with regret that I'm forced to announce the suspension of senior hockey in this community." The men in the audience shifted uncomfortably in their seats. If they were happy about the decision, their faces didn't show it. "Last year, the mill supported a senior club that was one of the best in the nation. But our team's general manager, in his zeal to win, broke several league rules and our team was suspended. Now he's our team's former general manager." There was a dramatic pause. "We allowed this man to import players at generous salaries. We found cushy jobs for them in the plant. But I regret to say they were mostly men of bad character. They drank and caroused and failed to do their jobs, on and off the ice. Now they've all been sent packing, along with the general manager and the coach. And I say good riddance to the lot of them."

"Geez, they fired the whole team," Marty muttered in surprise. "I thought hockey players were pretty good guys—most of them. These guys must have been real stinkers."

"Apparently most of them were," whispered Max.

Seymour cleared his throat and continued. "One of our players was excessively violent and put a player from another team in the hospital. Our man acted like a thug. Mr. Gray admires good, clean hockey. He will not tolerate players who act like hoodlums. What's more, he was shocked and embarrassed when our team was suspended for secretly breaking the salary cap imposed by the league. Gentlemen, Mr. Gray has had enough. He has asked me to tell you he's no longer willing to sponsor a hockey team. It's unfortunate, but this means the end of hockey in Indian River. And it's my opinion that we are well rid of a sport that has tarnished this town."

Max Mitchell bolted to his feet. "Mr. Seymour, you mean the end of senior hockey, don't you? What about junior hockey?" he asked. "You don't run into the same kind of problems you just mentioned with junior players. I've been told there's a pretty good nucleus in town for an excellent junior team. We should have a chance to play. Maybe we won't win any championships, but we'll be playing the game we love and it won't cost the plant more than a few dollars for ice time and equipment."

Max's passionate plea caught the attention of the younger men in the room. "You tell 'em, Max," one teenager shouted, clapping his hands together. Chubby Carlton whistled through his teeth, so loudly it caused Myron Seymour to wince and grit his teeth.

"Way to go, brother," whispered Marty. "That's got them squirming." Myron Seymour's face turned beet red with anger.

"A ridiculous suggestion, Mitchell," he blurted. "As a newcomer to town, perhaps you should learn to button your lip—until you get to know us." Max could feel his face turn red when he heard Seymour's insulting words. Seymour went on, happy to put a teenager in his place. "You actually expect the mill to finance a junior team, pay for and buy equipment for a club that has no teams to compete against?" He chuckled. "You'll wind up playing games of shinny amongst yourselves. The idea is preposterous." Seymour turned and smiled at the other board members. In an aside, he spoke softly but still loud enough for most to hear. "Tolerating foolish young men and their wild ideas is all part of my job," he sighed. "You may sit down now," he added, staring hard at Max.

But Max didn't sit down. He may have felt nervous arguing with his elders, but he wasn't finished with Seymour. "Why can't the fans pay for it—through gate receipts? As for a league to play in, we could enter our team in the Northern League—the senior league."

Seymour snorted like a frisky colt and almost

choked on a laugh. "Where you'd get clobbered in every game by older, better players," he sneered. "Now isn't that a bright idea? And who would pay to see the games? Have you thought of that, Mitchell? It would be a case of tough old veterans beating the snot... I mean beating the bejabbers out of kids who are still wet behind the ears." He couldn't resist pointing a finger and adding, "There are laws in this country about child abuse, beating up on kids," he snorted. "Some of you might be killed in a game. Who needs that? I'm talking about kids like you, Mitchell."

Max ignored the insult. "We may get clobbered, we may not," he countered, his voice beginning to rise. "But I promise you we'll play entertaining hockey. And we'll be in top shape so that we can outskate most of those old farts—pardon me, I mean those old fogies in the senior league. As for getting killed, some of the young guys who work in the mill are more apt to get killed on the job than in a hockey game. Just last month, didn't a teenage employee lose an arm to one of your big saws?"

"That's got nothing to do with hockey," Seymour spat back furiously. "Why don't you sit down and be quiet?" But Max remained standing, even though his knees began to tremble.

A buzz of conversation swept through the room. Obviously the thought of a junior team—kids under

20—replacing the suspended senior club hadn't occurred to anybody else in the hall. Even Harry Mitchell was surprised. He turned to gaze at his son, a look of pride and amusement on his face. He gave Max a big grin and a thumbs up.

Myron Seymour waved his hands to silence the crowd. "Quiet please. I think we've heard enough dissent. The fact remains, Mr. Gray is adamant," he stated. "There'll be no hockey, junior or senior, played in Indian River this season. That's final. Now I'm going to propose a motion…"

"No, wait, let me propose a motion," Max interrupted, waving a hand. "I propose that the hockey club seek permission to enter a junior team in the Northern League to replace our senior team. The club secretary can write the league officials and tell 'em how we feel. You just can't let hockey die in this town." Stunned into silence, Seymour stared at Max, his mouth open.

"I caught a big bass with a mouth like that once," Marty giggled, drawing a sharp nudge in the ribs from Max.

Max said, "All right fellas, you've heard the motion. I need a seconder."

Marty, seated next to him, leaped up and said, "I second the motion."

Seymour, confused and exasperated, desperately looked for a way out. "Wait a minute! Wait one minute!" he shouted, walking back and forth, stalling for time. Then he smiled sweetly, raised a finger and asked, "Are you boys registered with the Indian River Hockey Association? Because if you aren't..."

Max and Marty fished in their wallets and waved their membership cards in the air. The crowd hooted and laughed.

"So let's bring it to a vote," Max called out.

The older men in the crowd looked around nervously, uncertainly. But the young men in the room began to chant: "Vote! Vote! Vote!" Seymour noticed the young men scattered around the room outnumbered the oldtimers. He realized they were all members of the association because he was the one who had insisted they pay their annual dues of five dollars. He had no alternative. He had to call for a show of hands.

The petition proposed by Max was accepted by a margin of five votes. The oldtimers, most of them mill workers accustomed to obeying every edict handed down by Mr. Gray, were caught napping. They had come to bury hockey and a bunch of enthusiastic kids had resurrected it.

Seymour glared at Max Mitchell. "You're a newcomer to Indian River, Mitchell. I can see you don't understand how we do things here." He kept his voice level, but icy. "In my opinion, newcomers to town, like little children, should be seen and not heard."

"Oh, you're going to hear from us," Max replied. "What are you going to do—spank us? Make us stand in the corner?"

"You're in for a rude awakening, Mitchell. I think you've just bitten off more than you can chew."

"I just want to play hockey," insisted Max.

"Let me finish!" Myron Seymour roared. "It's obvious to all of us that you're a troublemaker. Well, if trouble is what you're after, trouble is what you'll get. I promise you that." Seymour threw some papers in a briefcase. He pulled on his expensive topcoat. He turned and threw Max a scowl. "Don't try to fool me with that Mr. Nice Guy approach. You're headed for a fall, Mitchell. A big one." Max just grinned and waved a mock salute at Seymour as the man stormed out of the room.

"Have a good night, Mr. Seymour," Marty shouted. "I love your suit. Did you buy it at Ringling Brothers?" But the slamming of the door drowned out Marty's final remark. "Hey, Mr. Seymour, be careful of the stairs out there. The cleaning lady just mopped them and they're a bit slippery…"

Crash! Thump! Bang!

"Sounds like somebody just took a tumble down the stairs," Max said, trying not to laugh. "I guess he didn't hear you."

"I tried to warn him," Marty shrugged. "And he said it was you who was headed for a big fall?"

CHAPTER 4
PLANNING THE NEXT MOVE

Max couldn't help feeling pleased with himself when he joined his new friends in a booth at Merry Mabel's Ice Cream Parlour after the meeting. The young men ranged in age from 15-year-old Marty Mitchell to 19-year-old Red Gadsby, a big, good-natured redhead who hadn't relished the thought of losing his final year of junior hockey.

"You sure made Seymour look sick," Red laughed, patting Max on the back. "I hear you pushed him down the stairs when he left the meeting."

"I did not," Max replied, chuckling, aware that Red was kidding him. "Don't start rumours, Red. People will believe them."

"Yeah, Max just wished he'd pushed old Seymour down the stairs," Marty chipped in.

"Anyway, ice cream's on me tonight," Red offered. "What'll you have, Marty?"

"How about one of those banana splits? I had

one the other day with three flavours of ice cream and loads of whipped cream. And three red cherries on top."

Red frowned and began counting the change in his hand. "I had a five-cent cone in mind. But I guess I can spring for a 25-cent sundae."

"You should never mention ice cream in front of my brother," Max told Red. "He drools like a baby at the sound of those two words."

"Good thing you're still in high school, Max," Jim McEvoy cautioned. McEvoy had been Gadsby's defence partner for years. "If you were a mill worker like some of us, and showed up that slippery Myron Seymour like you did tonight, you'd be out of a job tomorrow. Myron would see to it."

"Hey, I admit I was scared," Max said. "It's not easy to speak up to adults—especially when you're new in town."

"I wonder what'll happen next," said Chubby Carlton, with worry in his voice. "Looks like I may not get to play another season in goal. Seymour hates to be shown up. I wouldn't want to be in your shoes, Max." Chubby watched Marty dig a spoon into his banana split, then turned to Red. "Since you're buying, old pal, make mine a banana split, too, will you?"

"Get lost, Chubby. Any more sundaes for you and we'll have to carry you onto the ice with an earthmover this season."

A tinkling bell over the door announced the arrival of two more customers.

"Why, look who's here," said Red. "It's the boss's son and his pretty sister. Come have some ice cream, you two." Johnny Gray burst through the door accompanied by his 17-year-old sister Eileen. Johnny, who was 19, had befriended Max shortly after the Mitchells had arrived in Indian River. Johnny had recently donned overalls to learn his father's business from the ground up.

The boys told Johnny and Eileen what had happened at the meeting. Johnny roared with laughter. "When I'm boss, I'll have a job for you, Max," he said approvingly. "You can operate the big saw, the most dangerous one. Just be sure to count your fingers at the end of each shift."

His sister, petite and dark-haired with sparkling brown eyes, was Indian River High's valedictorian. Max found her to be attractive and smart, although it was said she had started dating Myron Seymour. Max couldn't help wondering what was so smart about that. Everybody liked Johnny and Eileen and the boys made room in the booth for them to join.

"What's this I hear about you telling Seymour to go fly a kite?" Johnny asked, nudging Max in the ribs and smiling broadly.

"What happened, Max?" asked Eileen, showing

snow-white teeth. "Seymour was so angry he could barely speak to me."

"Well, not much happened," Max told them. "Seymour—and your dad—thought we shouldn't have any hockey this season and I thought we should. We held a vote and hockey won out."

Oddly, Eileen didn't seem concerned about Myron Seymour's loss of face.

"It's so silly to try and stop hockey in Indian River," she said. "I told Myron that and I plan to tell my father as much. My brother and I love the game."

"I know you do," Max said. "And Johnny, I've heard how well you play the game. How about coming out and playing right wing for us? People tell me you had an outstanding career in that fancy prep school you attended."

"Gee, I'd love to play," sighed Johnny. "If I could sell my dad on that idea, I could sell fur coats in Florida. Or canoe trips over Niagara Falls. If you want to start a first-class row at our house, just mention hockey." He looked at his watch. "It's still early. Why not come over to the house right now and have it out with my dad?" He glanced at his sister. "Who knows what your hot-headed friend Myron's been telling him."

"I don't think Myron's really against hockey," she said. "He was just following orders. He's intimidated by Dad—like most people are."

Johnny said, "You bet he is," and grabbed Max by the elbow. "Come on, pal, let's go. You come too, Marty. Car's right outside. Eileen and I will lead you right into the den of the lion."

Max was nervous and Marty had little to say on the drive to the Gray mansion. Aside from the day Mr. Gray had presented the winning trophy to Max after the Big Race, the brothers had seldom seen the mill owner. He was a handsome, middle-aged man who wore tailored suits and well-polished shoes. Max said to his brother when they first saw Mr. Gray walking along Main Street, "That's the man who controls the future of almost everyone in Indian River." Now, sitting in the back seat of the mill owner's expensive limousine, he whispered to Marty. "I think I made a big mistake tonight. It was foolish of me to jump up and defy the wishes of Mr. Gray at the meeting. What if he decides to ruin Dad's newspaper? He could probably do it in a minute."

"I never thought of that," Marty whispered back. "Mom and Dad have put in long hours at the paper trying to make it a success. I sure hope he doesn't do that." Hard work was just beginning to pay off for the Mitchells when they had lived in Haileybury. There his dad had owned the *Haileyburian*—until the great fire had roared through town, destroying everything in its path, including the Mitchell's modest home and the newspaper office. Several people, caught by surprise, died in the inferno. On the night of the fire, the Mitchell family had fled to Cobalt, five miles away, but not before Max and Marty had been hailed as heroes for saving the lives of some townspeople. A few days later, like most of the burned-out residents, the Mitchells had come back to the town and begun to rebuild. Several of their friends and neighbours never returned. Of those who came back, the task of rebuilding houses and shops was almost too much—and too expensive. Not only did they stop subscribing to the newspaper Harry and Amy turned out each week, but they no longer needed to purchase advertising space in it. Even when proud shop owners came back to the scorched land covered with blackened rubble, it would take months before they would be back in business and be willing to advertise their merchandise in the *Haileyburian*. By then the newspaper would be bankrupt.

When the chance to buy the Indian River paper presented itself, Mr. Mitchell saw an opportunity he couldn't ignore. The owner was retiring after 50 years on the job. He was willing to sell at a bargain price but only to someone who would keep the integrity of the paper alive, someone who was fair-minded and skilled in covering community affairs in

Indian River. He found the ideal man—and an interested buyer—in Harry Mitchell. That was a few weeks ago.

When the car entered the long driveway that led to the Gray mansion, Max murmured to Marty, "Mr. Gray has the power to squash anyone in town if he feels like it. If he gets mad at us, and takes it out on the newspaper, we may have to move again." He sighed aloud.

"You okay back there?" Johnny Gray said from the front seat.

"Just fine, Johnny," Max said with a forced smile. "Say, this is one fine car, isn't it?"

They found Mr. Gray in his library. He had iron gray hair and the bluest eyes Max had ever seen. "Dad, this is Max Mitchell and his brother Marty," Johnny began. "Eileen and I met Max downtown and we persuaded him to come up here and have a big argument with you. Maybe the two of you can arm-wrestle each other across the dining room table. You up for it?"

Mr. Gray didn't answer at first, but he did favour his son with a fleeting smile. He shook hands with Max and Marty, looking them over. He frowned at Johnny and said gravely, "An argument about what?"

"About your favourite sport—hockey," said Eileen, grinning at her father.

He did not smile back.

"Hockey, is it?" he sighed. "Then there'll be no argument. I'm going to state my position once and for all and that'll be the end of the discussion. I don't hold any ill will toward you, Max. Myron told me how you swung that meeting over to your side tonight. That was clever of you and I admire clever people. You're smart and you're young and you're ambitious. Hockey must mean a lot to you."

"Not only to me, sir, but to most of the young men in town. You must have played the game. Surely you remember the joy of strapping on skates and flying across the ice with your teammates, trying to outscore the opposing team. Most young men, and lots of women too, know the sheer fun the game provides and we hate to be deprived of such joy."

"Let's get something straight. I'm not depriving you," Mr. Gray stated. "You had your meeting. Your side won the vote. The junior team will carry on. But understand this clearly: the company that I control will not support you."

"I'm sorry you look at it that way, sir. We're going to need all the help we can get."

Mr. Gray sighed. His eyes turned steely and hard. "It's not that I have anything against hockey, Max. Quite the contrary. But I'm a businessman. I'm in business to stay in business."

"I understand, sir."

Mr. Gray snorted. "No, I don't think you do. The players I hired last year turned on me. I treated them fairly. I paid them well. Just like I treat all my workers. But they wanted more money and threatened to bring in union organizers. Last year, our senior hockey team was outstanding—until it became involved in a major scandal. One of the players turned out to be a former pro playing under an assumed name. That was enough to have us kicked out of the league. Another player had a violent temper and deliberately broke an opponent's arm. A third was a thief who stole money from his own teammates. The whole experience sickened me."

Max tried to understand the mill owner's feelings. But he wasn't about to give up. "Sir, I'm not trying to tell you how to run your business. I just want to play hockey. The team I have in mind would be on its best behaviour at all times. They'll all be local boys and all of them amateurs, playing for the love of the game."

For the first time since the meeting began, Mr. Gray smiled. He had played some hockey in his youth. He remembered something about the love of the game. "Amateurs can't win in the Northern League," he said. "Especially teenage amateurs. The other teams are loaded with tough customers, bullies who break all the rules and defy the referees, who don't do anything about it. It's a waste of time to enter a team of juveniles against those packed clubs. Please, no more arguments. Max, I really believe you think a team of local boys can compete in the Northern League, perhaps even win a game or two. But you're sadly mistaken. It can't be done."

The meeting was over.

On their way to the car, Johnny said, "Sorry Max. You can see my dad is as stubborn as a mule."

"Johnny and I are still on your side, Max," Eileen said. She gave his arm a squeeze. "So don't give up."

"I won't," Max replied. "I may be almost as stubborn as your father. I plan to talk to the fellas. Get a team together. A good one, I hope. We all play the game because it's fun, it's not about business. In fact, most of the guys I know say hockey gives them more enjoyment than any other sport."

CHAPTER 5

MOULDING A TEAM

Sticks clashed over a bouncing rubber puck. A swift skater raced away with it. The big vaulted rink echoed to the occasional shouts and the bang of the puck against the sturdy white boards. A lanky winger swooped in on the defence, juggling the rubber, and then snapped a short pass across the ice to a teammate just as the defenceman lunged toward him. The puck hit the tape on Kelly Jackson's stick—but only for a second. He drew the other defenceman over, raced in, swept across the front of the net and backhanded the disc over the sprawling goaltender.

"Great play, Kelly!" Max Mitchell shouted. "That's the way to score goals."

He looked at the big clock at one end of the rink. He said to Kelly, "Hey, I wonder what's happened to our coach. He's never this late."

The rows of seats were empty. A sad-looking caretaker lounged against the gate, watching the Indians at practice. "A motley crew," he muttered to himself. "No big leaguers among this group. And those old jerseys they're wearing are pathetic. I've seen scarecrows that were better dressed."

Max divided the players into two teams, his three best forwards opposing the two top defencemen. He dropped the puck and skated to the bench as they scrambled after it. Johnny Gray was standing by the boards; his hands were thrust deep into the pockets of his overcoat. "What do you think, Johnny? How do they look?" Max asked.

"Fine. They look fine. And they've got spirit. But where's the coach?"

"That's what I'd like to know," Max said.

Steve Kennedy was the coach. Discovering him had been a stroke of good fortune for Max. Good coaches were rare, especially in small centres like Indian River. More than a score of ambitious youngsters had tried out for the team and Max had found it difficult to trim the squad. He knew he was in for trouble if he tried to coach players his own age while attempting to play at the same time. An older man was needed and suddenly appeared as if in answer to a prayer.

"Name's Kennedy," said the soft-spoken, middle-aged man who had arrived, following one of the early workouts. "I've handled a few junior teams in my time. Maybe you'd like a little help with this one."

"Not *the* Steve Kennedy?" gasped Max. "I've read about you in the papers. You took a team to the national title once, didn't you?"

"Yeah, but that was six years ago. You've got a good bunch of boys here. But some of them are pretty raw. I think I could smooth out some rough edges, get a little more out of them."

"That would be great, Mr. Kennedy. It would be fantastic." Max felt like turning handsprings. The famous Steve Kennedy was offering to help coach a group of unknown teenagers living in a North Country mill town.

"I came to work in the mill office a few weeks ago," the coach explained. "I've been away from the game for a couple of years. Lost my wife after a long illness and decided to move to Indian River. If you want me to help…"

"Help, Mr. Kennedy? Why not throw on some skates and start right now?"

"There's one more thing, Max. No more 'Mr. Kennedy.' You call me Steve, okay?"

In a few days, Coach Kennedy had worked wonders. He quickly won the respect of the players. He had an uncanny way of spotting weaknesses and correcting them. And the kids got a huge kick from what seemed to be his bottomless reservoir of witty sayings. One of the players Max had selected as a promising prospect, Kennedy promptly discarded after one or two practice sessions. "Every garden has some weeds, Max," Steve sighed. "You've got to pull them out. The kid can't take the rough play and never will. He's all flash and no substance," was the coach's verdict. "I'll give him the bad news."

"But Steve," Max protested. "He's so eager. He'll be heartbroken if you cut him."

Steve looked thoughtful. "Max, I know you like the kid and want him to succeed. So do I. But life is full of disappointments. Nothing dries sooner than tears. A coach can't hang on to players who will hurt, not help, the team. Even a small thorn causes festering. For every player who is bitter over being dropped, there's another who knows the thrill of being invited to play. The kid I cut will be upset and angry and so will his parents. They can beef all they want, but my decision stands. I know—and I think you know in your heart—I'm doing the right thing for the team. In hockey, coaches, like the players, can't be softies."

Max thought about it, and then nodded.

Steve laughed. "My father taught me some good lessons, Max. He used to say to me, 'Son, if you want to lead the band, you've got to turn your back on the crowd.' And once he told me, 'Even a kick in the behind brings you one step forward'."

"If you want to climb the ladder of success," Max chimed in, "you've got to start with the bottom rung."

Steve hooted. "You got it! You'll make a great coach one day, Max."

Max said, "Those are good sayings, I'll try to remember them."

The next day Steve Kennedy started working with Tom Ardath, one of the goaltenders Max had kept on the roster. Within a week, Ardath had developed into a netminder with skills almost equal to those of Chubby Carlton. "Ardath is quick. He's got all the tools. But I wonder about his attitude," Steve told Max. "I wouldn't be surprised if he causes some problems in the dressing room before long. We'll see."

Then he took Max aside and showed him a few on-ice tricks, some drills to work on. They were simple tips, ones that all pro players knew and amateur players tried to acquire. Max was very coachable, a fast learner. He gained confidence and thought his overall game had improved immensely in just a few days. Steve taught Max how to win more faceoffs and how to fake a pass to one winger while sliding it across the ice to another.

"Were you as good at faceoffs when you played?" Max asked Steve.

"Yep, very good. Not as good as Milt Schmidt of the Boston Bruins, but I found a way to beat him, too."

"How'd you do that?"

Steve chuckled. "I did something sneaky, something I never want to see you doing. Before the faceoff, I skated over to our bench and took a big swig of water. But I didn't swallow it. On the face-off, I leaned forward and squirted a mouthful of water into Schmidt's face just as the puck was dropped. The ref didn't see it, but it sure surprised Schmidt. I won a lot more faceoffs against him after that. I guess he never knew when he'd get another face wash." Max laughed so hard he almost fell off the bench.

One by one Coach Kennedy talked with the players. He ordered some to shorten their sticks by an inch or two. Others were taught how to cradle a pass, snap off a shot and finish their checks. All were told to keep their heads up and that winning the faceoff and controlling the puck were all-important. "Try not to panic and give the puck away—especially on the power play," he suggested. "Always remember hockey is a team game. When spiders unite and work as a team, they can tie up a lion." Some of the players chuckled. Others groaned. But over time they all came to see the truth of it. Goalies were shown how to cut down angles to the net, giving opposing shooters less of the twine to see.

One day Steve took Max aside. "They're getting better. Not world-beaters yet, but they're willing workers, determined to improve. You've got a much better team than anybody in town realizes. Remember that the homely colt often makes a powerful horse. It's going to be an interesting season. But playing against seniors is never easy. They hate to be shown up by teenagers."

Marty was sitting at rinkside, absorbed in a Hardy Boys book. He looked up when Max skated over. Max looked worried. Marty checked his watch. "He's 15 minutes late."

Max nodded. "I know."

Across the ice, a gate opened and Steve Kennedy skated out. His face was grim. He blew his whistle and called the players to centre ice. "Sorry I'm late, guys," he said hastily. "I had a meeting to attend. But we've got almost an hour left so let's go to work." He organized a brisk workout and every poorly executed play drew a whistle. "Let's do it again and let's do it right!" he barked. The coach's presence on the ice made a big difference in performance. There was more punch and energy shown, for every player was conscious that Steve's sharp eyes were on him, and that any letdown would draw a sharp rebuke.

The session ended with a half-dozen fast laps around the rink, the players whooping it up as they tried to outskate each other. Then it was off to the dressing room. There was a clatter of sticks and skates and a lot of verbal banter as the players crowded into the room and began peeling off their equipment. Steve Kennedy unlaced his skates, pulled on his shoes and stood up.

"I want your attention, men." The players stared up at him. They sensed something important was about to happen. "I like the way this team is coming together," he began. "You're all quick learners and you've all got the desire to improve. I believe in you, and to be successful, you've got to believe in yourselves. You've got another advantage over some teams you'll meet—a natural leader in Max. I don't have to tell you he's a gifted player, a natural and best of all—a team player. We could use one or two more good players, but there just aren't any more lads in Indian River who could make this club. Not to worry because some of you have shown great improvement. You've got the potential to surprise a lot of people. Now you have to go out there and do it."

"Coach, you sound like you'll never have a chance to bawl us out again," Max said.

"I won't," Steve replied. "I'm going away."

"No!" wailed the players. "How come?" shouted one. "What's going on?" demanded another.

"What rotten news," sighed Chubby Carlton, tossing a goal pad to the floor.

"You haven't been fired from the mill, have you?" Max asked. Steve's announcement came as a staggering shock. His first thought was that the company had dismissed Steve because of his association with the team.

"No, I haven't been fired. I've been transferred to the Chatsworth office. I'll be driving over there tomorrow. I hate to pull out now, just when the team is rounding into shape. And I can't commute because Chatsworth is 100 miles from here. It's just too far. I'm sorry boys, but orders are orders and a job is a job."

"I'll bet Myron Seymour had something to do with this," said Chubby. "Might as well hang up our skates and forget about the season."

"No, you won't!" Steve said sharply. "I want you men to win some games for me. I've given you a start. Max will act as playing coach. He knows enough about my methods to carry 'em out. I don't want to leave you with the idea this has all been a waste of time. I know how good you can be if you'll all stick together. How about it?"

"Okay!" the players roared. They rose to shake Steve's hand and wish him well. Max was the last one to speak with the coach.

"They did it deliberately," Steve said bitterly. "Chubby was right. They transferred me to get rid of me. Max, promise me you won't let them beat you, too."

"They're bound to try," Max answered grimly. "But this gives me some idea of what lengths they'll go to make life miserable for us. Looks like they're really determined to force us out of hockey. It's all about politics, not about a bunch of hometown kids having a little fun."

Steve started for the door. Then he turned and left Max with one final proverb. "Politics is like a rotten egg, Max. It stinks. Good luck, kid."

CHAPTER 6

A FINANCIAL CRISIS

Steve Kennedy's parting message to the Indians was not without its effect. When Max put the team members through their paces after school the following day, they listened to him without argument and flung themselves into the workout with as much enthusiasm and energy as they would have for Coach Kennedy. It was encouraging to know the team was behind him, even if the members of the hockey association and the town itself were not.

Max met Myron Seymour on the street after practice that day. "We've got to have some new equipment, Myron. We have no uniforms and the boys have been buying their own sticks. And our nets have holes in them. Can't you forget our differences and help us out?"

"Too bad," Seymour snorted. "What do you expect me to do about it? The hockey association has no money in the treasury."

"Let's call a meeting," Max suggested. "I'll talk to the members."

Seymour shrugged. "Well, we could do that, not that anything will come of it. How about tomorrow night?" he said.

This time Seymour was prepared for any surprises. The members who wanted to be rid of hockey hopelessly outnumbered the players. "Even their coach got fed up and quit on them," Seymour lied to his associates. "He said young Mitchell wouldn't listen to orders. Wanted to do everything his way."

When Max spoke passionately about the benefits of keeping the game alive, and suggested every member kick in a few dollars to provide equipment and uniforms, he was voted down. Every other fund-raising suggestion was vetoed. It became perfectly clear that the team could not expect any support, moral or financial, from the association.

"That's it, then," said Max, stemming his anger as he faced the old-line members. "You're determined to starve us out and see us fail. I'm telling you we won't fail. We'll find uniforms if we have to knit them ourselves and we'll find sticks if we have to make 'em from tree branches."

Seymour roared with laughter. "That'll be a pretty sight," he shouted at Max. "You better start climbing trees and whittling those branches because your first game is in Chatsworth on Saturday night. You better call over there and cancel the game."

Max was able to control his impulse to tell Seymour to take a flying leap in the lake. But his blue eyes were blazing when he snapped, "Don't you worry about it. We'll be there," he promised.

"I doubt that," laughed Seymour. "But if you do go I suggest you start early. It's a mighty long walk." Most of the members laughed along with Seymour.

"We'll play in Chatsworth," Max repeated, as he headed for the door. "And we won't be walking there." Immediately, he began to wonder if he'd spoken too hastily. Chatsworth was 100 miles away and a part of the highway between the towns had recently washed away, forcing cars and trucks to make long detours. His father had written about the highway disaster in the *Review* and how it would take many days to repair the road. That left only one way to get to Chatsworth—by train.

The players gathered in Merry Mabel's Ice Cream Parlour to discuss ways and means of raising money for the train fare to Chatsworth. Max and three of the other players offered to pay their own way. Max still had a few dollars left from the prize money he'd won in the Big Race. The rest of the team members admitted they were flat broke. Max did some figuring. "We've got to raise 36 dollars for fares. We can save on hotel rooms if we stay up all night and come back on the early morning train."

"Yeah, we can do that," said Chubby. "I'll bring a deck of cards."

"What about meals?" someone asked.

"Any objection to packing lunches?"

"We can do that too," said Chubby, a young man known for his voracious appetite.

"We can all take turns helping you carry your lunch bucket, Chub," Kelly Jackson quipped. "It's bound to be heavier than your goal pads."

"But how do we raise the 36 bucks we need?"

"We'll canvas the town," Max suggested. "Surely there are enough fans left in Indian River to put up some money."

They went to work but soon discovered that men who worked in the mill didn't dare risk the company's displeasure. Merchants who counted on company business shied away from any suggestion of supporting the hockey team.

"Boys, I'd like to help you out and I would under normal conditions. But Myron Seymour was in to see me. You know how it is...." They raised exactly 17 dollars and 35 cents.

There was gloom in the dressing room when the players met again. Most of them were ready to throw in the towel. Even Max's confidence was badly shaken. Then the door opened and Johnny Gray walked in. "Well, how did you boys do? I don't see a lot of cash spilling out of your pockets."

"Looks like the Chatsworth game is off, Johnny." Max said. "We can't get far on a little more than seventeen bucks."

"I guess not," said Johnny. "You know my respected parent would cut me off without a dime if I played hockey with you men. But maybe I can assist in another way, like arranging a private railway car to get you to Chatsworth."

"Private car?" yelped one of the boys. "What the heck are you talking about?"

"Listen, this will be our little secret. I have a pal in the shipping department at the company," Johnny said. "And he has some friends with the railwaymen. They are all hockey fans and they're willing to look the other way from time to time. There's a freight train leaving from the mill siding and bound for Chatsworth tomorrow afternoon at three o'clock. I'll lead you to a place where you can hop aboard." And with a big grin on his face, he turned and marched out of the room.

The following afternoon, Myron Seymour and two mill executives turned up at the railway depot. They watched a passenger train bound for Chatsworth roll into the station. A few minutes later, the porter shouted "All aboard" and the train pulled out. Nobody got on or off the train.

Seymour chuckled and patted an associate on the back. "I didn't see any hockey players climb aboard, did you? What a shame. Looks like the local boys lose their first game in Chatsworth by default," he said. "I hope that brash Mitchell kid knows that if his team loses two games by default, that's it. The Indians will be kicked out of the league."

"That young man is a troublemaker and stubborn as a mule with a toothache," the associate said. "But I don't see how his team will default two games in a row. Their next game is on home ice, isn't it?"

"Just you wait and see," Seymour laughed. "I've got a big surprise for them." He pulled his associates closer and told them of his plans, how he'd shock the Indians into submission. There was no question the Indians would lose two games in a row by default.

"Well, Myron, I'll say this for you," said an admiring voice. "When you set out to scuttle someone's plans, you do it right. Your idea will sink the young rebels' hopes for sure."

"I'm full of good ideas, men," Seymour boasted. "That's why I expect to run the mill someday."

A hoot of a freight train was heard in the distance, over on the siding that ran from the mill. Seymour and his friends, if they heard it at all, thought nothing of it.

There was plenty of activity on the siding. Young men scrambled through the open door of a boxcar and perched themselves on top of huge rolls of milled paper. A couple of retired mill workers, willing to act as chaperones, climbed aboard too. Within minutes the car began to roll, slowly at first. The players were beginning an unconventional trip to Chatsworth. Two latecomers were hauled by teammates into the boxcar. Everyone was there except Chubby Carlton, the goaltender.

"Where the heck is he?" moaned Kelly Jackson. "We can't play in Chatsworth without a goaltender."

"Here he comes!" someone yelled. They rushed to the open door and saw Chubby floundering through the deep snow of the railway embankment, lugging his heavy goal pads.

"Come on, Chubby," Red Gadsby yelled as he knelt down and reached out a helping hand. Chubby tripped and fell, got up again. He stumbled and almost lost his footing. For a moment Max thought he would fall under the rolling wheels. But Chubby recovered and lunged toward the open door. Max and Red grabbed his arms and hauled him aboard. When he was safely inside and sitting on his goal pads, everyone laughed and pounded Chubby on the back.

"Your parents aren't going to approve of this," one of the retired mill workers said. "What did they say when you told them?"

"I told them we were going to Chatsworth by car,"

Red Gadsby said. "I just didn't mention boxcar."

Most of the boys had told their parents the truth—at Max's urging. "But be sure to tell them we have two adult chaperones coming along to look after us," he had said. "Both are former hockey players."

It was a full five minutes before Chubby could catch his breath and explain his tardiness. "The caretaker at the rink wouldn't give me a key to the dressing room," he gasped. "He said Myron Seymour had ordered him not to. I had to slip through a window to grab my gear. Then I ran like heck, and you all know I'm no runner." Suddenly, a look of horror passed across Chubby's face. "Oh, no," he wailed. "I left it back at the rink."

"What, Chub, your goal stick?" Max asked. "No, you didn't. We hauled it aboard."

"Worse than that," Chubby responded, a tear spilling from one eye. "I left my lunch pail back there. Now I'm going to starve to death."

CHAPTER 7

THE GAME IN CHATSWORTH

"We made it, Steve, and it was fun. Chubby moaned and groaned all the way about his lost lunch pail, but we shared some sandwiches with him and that kept him quiet. Now we're hoping you can help us out tonight. We want you back behind the bench." It was an hour before game time and Max was sitting in the visitors' dressing room in the Chatsworth Arena. Sitting next to him was Steve Kennedy, his mentor.

Steve looked at Max. "Seems to me your team already has a good coach, Max. And the more experience you get, the better. The players all look up to you now and my coming back might prove to be a distraction, especially for just one game. But I'll tell you what I'll do for you. I'll sit in the first row of seats, right behind your bench. If you call for advice, I'll be there for you. But I don't think you'll need it."

"A lot of people back home are going to think we're insane, doing what we're doing," Max said grimly. "They're going to laugh and say, 'We told you so,' if we lose big to the Beavers, not to mention the other senior clubs."

"So what?" Steve asked. "People laughed at the Wright brothers, didn't they? They said flying was for fools and both would fall to their deaths. What you're attempting is admirable. Remember that a wise man makes his own decisions; an ignorant man follows public opinion. My father used to say to me, 'You've got to do your own growing, no matter how tall your grandfather was.'" Max chuckled.

Just then Chubby entered the room, lugging his goal pads. "Hi, Steve," he said, rushing over to shake hands with the former coach. "Great to see you. You gonna be coaching us tonight?"

"No, I'm here to cheer for you. But I'll be right behind your bench in case Max gets flustered and forgets how many players make up a team."

Chubby smiled, and then grew serious. "I heard some of the Beavers mingling with their fans beside the concession stand a few minutes ago—I had to stop and get a couple of hot dogs to settle my stomach—and they were bragging about how many goals they were going to throw into my net tonight. They said, like 20, maybe."

"Every ass likes to hear himself bray, Chubby,"

Steve said, rising to leave. "Now I'm going to find my seat. Good luck tonight. And remember, boys, there's no luck where there's no discipline. See you later—after you win."

When the teams lined up for the game, Butch Taylor, the Chatsworth captain, sneered at Max. "That's a pretty tattered jersey you've got on, bud. Makes the league look bad." Taylor puffed out his chest. "See, we've got new ones. Great colours, huh?"

"And a lot of them," Max said, agreeably. "The last time I saw colours like that was at the circus. The clown was wearing them. Besides, anyone can put a silk shirt on a mule, but it's still a mule."

"Huh? What's that supposed to mean?"

"You figure it out, Taylor."

"A wise guy, huh?" snarled the opposing centre-man. "Well, you guys look like hobos in those ratty uniforms."

"We're saving our new ones," Max said, smiling.

"Saving 'em? What for?"

"For the playoffs. What else?"

Taylor snorted, showing some missing teeth. "As if you'll make the playoffs. That's a good one. With all those green kids in your lineup?"

"Young wood makes a hot fire," Max shot back, recalling words Steve had once uttered.

"Huh?"

The referee dropped the puck and Max snapped it

up and broke away from Taylor's awkward lunge. Taylor's stick struck a blow just above his knee. He winced, stumbled and almost went down. Max sent a pass across the ice to Kelly Jackson who was immediately slammed into the boards by a husky Chatsworth defenceman. The game was underway and the Indians knew immediately they were in for a rough evening.

In the warm-up period before the game, they'd been subjected to hoots and derisive laughter from the stands. Their worn, tattered uniforms and battered equipment was in sharp contrast to the colourful new uniforms worn by the Chatsworth Beavers. The first five minutes of play, however, showed the Beavers and their fans that Max and his mates were out to make a game of it. After Max was slashed and Kelly Jackson was boarded in the opening seconds of play, while the referee "appeared" to have something in his eye, the Indians unleashed a torrid attack, ripping into the Beavers with everything they had. The Indians were faster and younger than the Beavers and they ripped a number of shots at Bouncing Bobby Boone, the startled Chatsworth goaltender. With Max leading the way, the Beavers were caught by surprise and were all but swept off their skates by the kids from Indian River.

Then Taylor, the Beaver captain, snared a loose puck and sped away with it, Max right on his heels.

Taylor was about to shoot when Max deftly hooked the puck away, turned and raced down the ice with it. The Beaver defence closed in on him, determined to flatten the Indians' star player. But Max swung sharply to his right, drawing one defenceman toward him. He slipped a quick pass across to Peewee Halloran. The little winger flashed through the opening, swooped in on the goalie and faked a shot to the corner of the net. Bobby Boone sprawled across the crease, lunging for a puck that wasn't there. With a smile, Halloran lifted the puck into the upper corner of the net and the red light flashed. Steve Kennedy had shown Halloran how to make that move.

The Chatsworth spectators were stunned. This young team from Indian River had speed and grit and an attitude that said, "We may be young, but we won't be pushed around."

Max, Kelly and Peewee skated furiously and almost clicked for a second goal when Max rifled a shot off the goal post. The Beavers, expecting an easy victory against the teenagers, couldn't find their skating legs. They hadn't practiced very hard for the opening game; they had thought they would win by default. Now they simply couldn't get going.

A Beaver defenceman swung around his team's net and lumbered down the ice. Peewee Halloran stood in his way and lashed out with his stick, knocking the puck away. It came right to Max, who spun quickly, eluding a bodycheck from Taylor, who once again slashed him across the knees. Max scooped up the disc, and flashed in on the crouching goalie. He drove the puck to the upper corner. Boone's big glove flew up, but not in time. The puck whipped into the twine and fell to the ice. The Indians led by two goals midway through the first period.

Exasperated, the Beavers' coach hastily called his men over for a huddle at the bench. The referee, who had failed to call three or four obvious penalties against the Beavers—including the two slashes Taylor laid on Max, let the coach take all the time he needed.

"We'll get no favours from that ref," Kelly Jackson snorted. "He's got a brother on the Beavers."

During the timeout, Chubby Carlton angered the crowd by hollering, "Can't see much of the game from down here." He yawned and leaned against the crossbar as though he was going to take a nap. The crowd booed.

Taylor, who once had a tryout with the famed Montreal Canadiens, glowered at Max when they lined up again. "You guys must think you're 60-minute men," he snarled.

Max grinned at him. "We're in pretty good shape," he admitted, "especially when we play against fat, old has-beens."

"Smartass," grunted Taylor. "They'll have to carry you guys out of here on stretchers."

Coach Steve Kennedy had always stressed the importance of backchecking and a strong defence and Max could hear him urging the Indians from his rinkside seat, "Come back, skate back!" While the Beavers tried to take the offensive, the Indians backchecked them to a standstill. Rushes were broken up and passes were intercepted. Red Gadsby and Jim McEvoy, standing their ground on defence, laid out some punishing bodychecks.

An angry Butch Taylor got possession of the puck in the neutral zone and leaped ahead with it. He was off like a streak of lightning, catching the two Indian defencemen off guard. They scrambled back as Taylor barrelled through and whipped a bullet-like drive at Chubby Carlton. Chubby threw out his leg and stopped Taylor's blast with his pad, but the puck rebounded right back onto Taylor's stick. The fans, sensing a goal, leaped up and roared. But all that noise-making came too soon. When Taylor snapped up the puck and fired, Chubby dove headlong in its path and smothered the shot. Then he saw the puck squirt away from him, rolling toward the open net. Taylor took a vicious cut at it and missed. Chubby reached back. His glove closed over the puck just as it was about to cross the goal line. He swept it out of danger—out to the corner where Red Gadsby snared it and fired it off the boards and up into the neutral zone.

The Beavers came right back, attacking relentlessly. They shook off checks and peppered Chubby with shots. He was up and down like a yo-yo on a string. But he threw his stout body in front of every drive. When the whistle signalled the end of the period, he lay on the ice on his back, completely exhausted. "Thanks, boys," he groaned when his mates hauled him to his feet and led him to the dressing room. "Boy, if we can only win this game, the fans will have to get behind us in Indian River."

When they skated out for the second period, the Indians faced a different team. The Beavers' coach had given his team a tongue-lashing during the intermission and the Chatsworth forwards went straight to the attack at the drop of the puck. But they were met by cool, hard-checking defencemen and forwards who fought them for every inch of ice. Time and again, Chatsworth's passing plays were broken up. When the Beavers did gain the blue line, Red Gadsby and Jim McEvoy laid into them with solid body checks. Occasionally a player broke through and drilled a shot at Chubby Carlton. But the goalie turned back every drive. The second line of the Indians had trouble coping with the pressure. More often now, the Beavers crashed through that battered, weary trio of forwards. They began breathing down Chubby Carlton's neck. The Chatsworth crowd, expecting a goal, howled encouragement.

Taylor skated out, fresh from a long rest. From a faceoff, he grabbed the puck and turned to circle his team's net. Taylor gathered speed and swung back down the ice. He was a speedster and by the time he reached centre ice he was flying. Max and Kelly Jackson closed in on him but he altered course and burst between them. He eluded a hip check from a defenceman and swooped down on Chubby like a hawk after a field mouse.

His shot was a blinding drive that Chubby gamely leaped for. But it tore into the twine behind him as Taylor flashed by, slipping an elbow into Chubby's face as he passed. The goaltender went flopping into the net, howling in pain while Taylor raised his arms in triumph. The Beavers now trailed by one.

The Chatsworth crowd yelled with glee. "Tay-lor! Tay-lor! Tay-lor!" they shouted. It had been their first opportunity to rejoice and they made the most of it.

Max helped Chubby to his feet and complained to the referee about the elbow to the goalkeeper's face. The referee retrieved the puck from the net and snarled, "Don't argue with me, kid. Taylor never touched him. Your guy is faking. I should give him two minutes for diving."

With Max at his side, Chubby skated in small circles until his head cleared.

"Someday," Max said to his goaltender, "someone is going to invent a face mask to protect you goalies from flying pucks and elbows. Maybe you should do it, Chub."

"Nah, it'll never happen," Chubby replied, wiping sweat from his brow. "Goalies would be called sissies if they wore masks. Just like they'd call you forwards sissies if you wore helmets. I'm okay now, ready to play."

Max skated slowly back to centre ice. He took his time about it, stopping to have a word or two with his wingmen. He wanted to give his mates time to settle down.

Chubby then discovered one of his skate laces had come loose and he threw off his gloves and knelt to tie it. It was an old trick, but it gave the Indians a few more seconds to collect themselves.

"Good strategy, Max," Steve Kennedy called out, cupping his hands to his mouth.

"Come on, quit stallin'," the referee barked and moved in to drop the puck. Max won the draw from Taylor and darted toward the enemy goal. He passed the puck to Jackson, who was herded into the boards by a burly Chatsworth defenceman. Max went into the slot, hoping for a pass. Suddenly, Jackson kicked the puck free and sent the disc spinning across to him. Max pounced on it; turned to shoot and was sent sprawling, knocked dizzy by a thunderous check.

"Two minutes for charging," shouted the referee. He sent a mean-looking defenceman to the box. The penalized player skated past Max, who was still on his knees. "That was just a love tap," he chuckled. "Come back my way again and I'll really work you over."

"You've got to catch me first," snapped Max. "Have a nice rest in the penalty box."

Max stayed out for the power play, trapped the puck on the faceoff and fed a hard pass back to Halloran, playing the point. But Halloran was tired and lost the puck to a Beaver penalty killer who banged it past him and broke away with it.

Halloran turned in pursuit and soon caught up, forcing the puck carrier to the boards. But his opponent stopped sharply. Surprised by the move, Halloran crashed heavily into the boards. He went down in a heap. "What next?" Max said aloud as he raced over to help Halloran to his feet. Halloran winced as he put his weight on his right ankle. But he insisted on staying in the game.

"I'm all right," he muttered. "Let's get going."

But when play resumed, Max could see clearly that Halloran wasn't all right. A Beaver winger raced past him with ease, and fired point-blank on Chubby Carlton. Chubby got his stick on the puck, deflecting it high into the crowd. Max sent Halloran to the bench and Marshall jumped over the boards to replace him.

"Good move," Steve Kennedy said, approvingly.

Chubby Carlton made half a dozen sensational saves before the period ended. Max could hardly believe the Beavers hadn't taken the lead. He led his players to the dressing room and tried to ignore the booing and taunting from the crowd. One more period left to play.

Max stood by the open dressing room door. "Twenty minutes, men. We've got to hold on for another 20 minutes. If we can do it, we'll have proved that a junior club can win in this league. And we'll have the town behind us for the rest of the winter."

Just then, the referee and two linesmen passed by the open door. Chubby Carlton saw them, winked and said to his mates in a loud voice, "Here's a riddle for you, men. What has six eyes and can't see?" The three officials stopped short, and like the players, waited for the answer. Chubby shouted out, "Three blind mice. Get it?"

The officials moved on down the hall, not sure whether or not they'd been insulted. Then the referee, not known for his sense of humour, returned to the open door and called out, "Here's another riddle for you, fellas. What lies on its back 100 feet in the air?" Before anyone could reply, he gave the answer. "A dead centipede."

A roar of laughter filled the room as Chubby got up and gently closed the door in the referee's smiling face. "That's enough levity," he said to his mates. "I can see that Max wants us to be serious. And he's right, of course. So let's put our game faces back on."

CHAPTER 8
THIRD PERIOD HEROICS

Max Mitchell didn't feel very confident when the Indians skated out to face the Beavers for the third period. Peewee Halloran's ankle had swollen to an alarming size during the intermission and he was done for the night. Fred Marshall would have to take over on left wing and the Indians were desperately short of reserves. Even burdened with these obstacles, Max knew his club had something the Beavers lacked—loyalty and teamwork. The total absence of hometown support had knitted the Indians together. He could bank on every one of them to fight to the final whistle.

The Beavers skated out. Some of them looked sullen. Max guessed that their coach had given them another lengthy tongue-lashing between periods.

"One goal isn't going to be enough," Max told Kelly Jackson as they circled the ice. "We're going to be dragging our tails for the final ten minutes. We've got to score at least once more."

"We will, Max, we will," said Kelly, a lanky, sandy-haired kid and a perpetual optimist. "If we can score in the first few minutes, it'll take the steam right out of the Beavers."

Max crouched over the faceoff. "Bet your coach ripped into you," he told Taylor, whose head was just inches away. "Here we are without a manager, coach or trainer, and with only a couple of subs, and we're making you bigshots look foolish. You beginning to feel the pressure, Taylor?"

"Aw, shut up," Taylor growled.

Max's goading had upset the opposing centre, so he was slow to react when the third period began. Max snared the puck, poked it ahead and flew straight at the Beaver defence. Marshall and Jackson hustled to keep up. Max lanced a long, looping shot into the corner end boards and raced in after the rebound. The puck came right to his stick and he drilled it at the Beaver goalie. He saw it just in time and kicked it out. By then, Jackson was roaring in, caught up to the loose puck and let it drive while in full stride. The goalie was lucky to take it on his pads, but, off balance, he cleared it badly. Marshall snared the puck on his stick, but was bowled over by a defenceman. While falling, Marshall skimmed the puck over to Max, who smoked in another shot. Another Beaver save—and a great one.

Max grabbed the rebound and out of the corner of his eye he saw Red Gadsby steaming in from his defence position. He faked a shot on goal, the Beaver goalie flopped to block it as Max calmly sent a perfect pass to Gadsby. Red let go from about 20 feet and the puck tore into the net. The red light flashed. The quick goal stunned the Beavers and their fans.

The Beavers were livid with anger now. They had assumed the shabby little crew from Indian River would be content to play defensive hockey in the third period and try to cling to their lead.

From the ensuing faceoff, the Beavers picked up the pace and tore in with a vicious, speedy attack. But the whole team had been built around Taylor because he was the playmaker, and if he couldn't give or receive passes, their number-one line was disorganized. Taylor was the puppeteer who pulled all the strings, but Max made sure his hands were tied by staying right at his elbow on every shift. He talked to him, riled him and infuriated him. Conceit was Taylor's biggest weakness. "They told us you were good, Taylor, almost good enough for the Canadiens. That's a laugh. We're skating rings around you tonight."

Time after time, Max intercepted Taylor's passes. He stole the puck off his stick three times. It messed up the Beaver attack and it messed up Taylor's mind. He swung his stick at Max in anger and drew a penalty. Meanwhile, time was ticking off the clock.

Midway through the period, the Indians were feeling exhausted. One by one, the Beavers were beginning to break through the defence. But these were mainly solo efforts and Chubby Carlton handled the shots with ease.

On the bench, Max turned to Steve Kennedy. "Any thoughts, coach?"

"You know what to do, Max," Steve answered, leaning forward. "Have your players lob the puck down the ice, over the heads of the Beavers. Or play it off the boards—hard. But no passes up the middle because they're easily intercepted. And look for a surprise scoring chance. The Beavers won't be expecting any more offence from you."

The Indians, leg-weary and gasping for breath, hung on tenaciously. They lobbed the puck down the ice two or three times. With five minutes to play, the Beavers took control. They slammed rubber at Carlton from a dozen angles. When Jim McEvoy turned and fell down exhausted, a Beaver wingman flipped the puck over Chubby's shoulder and into the net, reducing the Indians' lead to one. The Beavers smelled victory now. The visitors were plainly losing energy. The fans cheered when Red Gadsby drew a penalty for tripping. Out came the Beavers' power play, led by Taylor. The Beavers waded in when the puck was dropped. Chubby stopped a shot with his stick and was about to fall on the puck when he heard Max cry out, "Here, Chubby!" Max had turned up ice along the boards. Chubby sent a pass soaring in the air and it landed just ahead of Max's flashing blades. But his blades seemed to be weighted down with lead. And the rink appeared to be a mile long. But there was only one defenceman protecting Bobby Boone.

Max knew he'd never have a better chance to score. He dug in, moving faster. Taylor was right on his heels, hacking at his legs and stick. Max drove his skates into the ice and Taylor fell back. The big defenceman loomed in front of him and tried to slam him into the ice with a vicious check. Max dodged the blow and the blueliner stumbled and fell into the boards with a crash that shook the building. Taylor was back, all over him, was about to tackle him. Max snapped off a wrist shot. The puck struck the goalie high on the chest, then dropped in front of him. Max and Taylor raced for it, but Max got there first—just as Taylor lashed out with his stick and tripped him. Max flew through the air, saw a small opening between the goalie's skates, reached down with the blade of his stick and tipped the puck through it. The red light flashed. He heard Taylor's curse and the goalie's groan. The Beavers knew at that moment that the game was lost.

Moments later, the Indians skated off with a hard-earned four to two victory. They flung themselves on the dressing room benches and on the floor, knowing they had just stunned everybody with one of the biggest upsets in the history of the Northern League.

Steve Kennedy, his face flushed, was there to congratulate his former charges. He doled out compliments and said, "I'm so proud of you, boys." Then he turned to leave.

Chubby called out to him, "Hey, Steve, haven't you got a final word of advice? An old proverb? Anything?"

Steve laughed and said, "My father used to say, 'Nothing is impossible to willing hearts and young legs.' And you fellows have them both. You're going to go far this season, mark my words." The door closed behind him and he was gone.

A few minutes later, to the Indians' surprise, Aggie Kirkham, coach of the Beavers, entered their dressing room. He had been around the hockey wars for a long time and he knew how to take defeat gracefully. "How you lads did it, I don't know, but you amazed us tonight. Your win should take a little conceit and arrogance out of my boys." Looking at Max, he said, "Good work, tonight, big fellow. That last goal of yours was a marvel. It took the heart out of us. What's this I hear about them treating you badly back in Indian River?"

"We'll survive," Max said, too exhausted to

explain much more.

"And I hear you got here by boxcar. That shows spunk but it's also very dangerous. Not a good idea. How are you going to get back home?"

Max shrugged. "We've got a few dollars," he answered.

"Not nearly enough, I'd guess," said Kirkham. He rose and held out his hand. Max shook it and looked down to discover the rival coach had slipped him some bills. "That should be enough to get your team safely home—in a day coach," he said, smiling. "And you can sleep right here in this dressing room tonight. The old pot-belly stove will keep you warm." The players who'd been listening cheered Kirkham.

"Thanks, coach," they shouted, coming over to shake his hand.

"If your hometown fans don't get behind you now, they don't deserve a hockey club," Kirkham said. "You've got a nicely balanced hockey team with great spirit, but you need a couple more subs."

"We'll find 'em," said Red Gadsby.

"You'll need 'em for your home game against the Wolverines. I'm sure they're going to be the team to beat. Picked men, all of them. And tough. By the way, where was your coach tonight?"

Max grinned. "Steve Kennedy? Oh, he was transferred here to Chatsworth and had to resign as our coach. He came by before the game to say hello. I asked him to coach us tonight but he declined. He said I'm the player-coach now and that's the way it should be. But he's still our biggest fan."

"Well, he sounds like a smart man," Kirkham said. "He left the club in good hands."

"He's a great hockey man," Max said. "He moulded our team right from the start."

When Kirkham left, Gadsby turned to Max. "He's a good guy, that Kirkham. I guess not everybody is against us after all."

The players threw more wood in the pot-belly stove and found places on the floor to sleep. They threw on jackets and coats and used their jerseys as pillows.

"I guess it's my responsibility to get you up in time to catch the morning train," Max said, rummaging in his hockey bag. "I brought along a special alarm clock and it's in here somewhere."

At six a.m. the players were awoken by a strange odour, the vilest smell imaginable. Around him, Max watched his teammates jumping up, holding their noses and gagging. They scrambled their gear together.

"What's that stench?" someone snorted. "Did a skunk get in here during the night? Smells like a warehouse full of farts. Let's get out of here. Yuck!"

The players hurried out of the dressing room.

Chubby Carlton was the last to leave and he turned to see Max chuckling as he closed the door. "What's so funny?" Chubby asked suspiciously.

"Oh, nothing," Max said with merriment in his eyes. "I told the guys I'd get 'em up. I didn't tell them I'd use a stink bomb to do the trick."

CHAPTER 9

RINK PROBLEMS

If the Indians figured their dramatic victory over Chatsworth would be the subject for much rejoicing at home, the notion was quickly dispelled when the players stepped off the morning train. They had slept overnight on the floor of the dressing room in the Chatsworth arena and were stiff and sore after their trip.

"You fellas been away?" asked old Grady Mortson, the station agent.

Jim McEvoy glared at him. "We were playing hockey in Chatsworth."

"That so?" said Mortson walking away. "Well, Chatsworth's a nice town." He didn't even ask who'd won.

The players scattered to their homes and boarding houses. Max went straight to school and found Marty waiting for him outside his classroom. Marty quickly put down The Melted Coins—the Hardy

Boys book he'd been reading. He was anxious to hear all the details.

"I wish I'd been there," Marty said. "I could have been the stick boy. By the way, I played in goal for the high-school team while you were gone. Got a shutout, too."

"That's great, Marty. Another year or two and you'll be ready to take over for Chubby."

"I'm ready now," Marty said confidently. "And you should know it."

At school, at the mill, everywhere in town, hardly anyone had heard about the Indians' triumph over Chatsworth. Hockey had been forgotten. Harry Mitchell helped by asking Max about the game and putting a brief mention of it in the *Review*. But he was concerned that the players had hitched a ride to Chatsworth in a boxcar.

"Your mother and I agree that getting to games that way is far too dangerous," he told Max. "Someone could have fallen and been badly hurt. I can't let you do that again."

"But, Dad, we were pretty desperate," Max argued.

"I know, but you simply can't travel that way, even with chaperones," his father insisted. "And I'm sure I speak for the other parents. Max, as the team leader, you are expected to set a good example for the others. Stealing rides in boxcars isn't my idea of a good example." When Max thought about it, he knew his father was right. He promised never to sneak into a boxcar again.

Over dinner that night, his father said, "Max, you know I have to be somewhat discreet when it comes to what I print in the *Review*. Too much hockey in the paper and Mr. Gray and Myron Seymour can make things rough on me."

Max said he understood. "Look, we don't expect a lot of publicity, Dad. Don't take any risks on our account. We're only fighting to play because we love the game." The telephone rang and he dashed for it. "Hello?"

"Max, this is Eileen Gray."

"Hi, Eileen."

"I'm late with my congratulations, but I wanted to tell you I'm so happy your team won last night. Red Gadsby tells me you were the star of the game. I wish I could have been there."

"Actually, Red was the star. He's a great defence-man. And Chubby was superb in goal. Listen, Eileen, we play the Wolverines here on Tuesday night. You can see that game."

There was a pause. Then Eileen said, "Max, that's why I'm calling. Myron was here a short time ago. He told me there's a hockey association meeting tonight. I overheard him tell somebody on the phone that it was all hush-hush. But I think they're planning to keep you from getting ice time at the arena for Tuesday's game. I thought you should know there's something brewing. Myron will be furious with me for telling you about it. But then, I'm furious with him."

Max thanked her for the information, hung up and raced to the door, throwing on his jacket as he went. Marty, sensing his brother was in more trouble, was right behind him.

"I think they're planning to close the rink on us," he told Marty. "I should have anticipated this. I should have studied the rink contract instead of assuming that everything was in order."

He and Marty found the meeting room and barged in without knocking. Myron Seymour was at the head of the table. An overweight man named Barlow, a white-haired old gentleman named Wyatt and a quiet little man named Carstairs surrounded him. They were all members of the arena executive committee and were employees or former employees of Mr. Gray. Heads turned and eyes widened with astonishment when Max and Marty boldly walked in.

Seymour rose and said, "Hey, this is a private meeting. What are you two doing here?"

"I think we need to be here," Max answered. Max wasn't quite sure of his ground so he asked, "Is the hockey club's contract for ice time in the rink up for renewal? If so, we want to renew."

"It was," Seymour said, folding his arms and grinning at his friends on the committee.

"I'd like to know if it was renewed on last year's terms?"

"We can give you that information, boy," cackled old Wyatt. "But you're not going to like it."

Barlow's voice boomed out. "You're the young know-it-all who's been trying to show us oldtimers where to get off. Well, it's our turn now." He picked up a sheet of paper and handed it to Max. "Here's the new contract, sonny. Read it and weep."

Max read it. His lips grew tight but he didn't weep. The terms were outrageous—impossible to meet. They called for a guarantee of 150 dollars per game and 50 percent of the gate receipts, plus 15 dollars an hour for practice time.

Marty, looking over his brother's shoulder, piped up. "Why, you mean old goats," he yelped.

Max threw the paper in front of Wyatt. He turned to Seymour. "You're obviously behind this. If you're looking for a fight, you're about to get one. We've built up a nice little team, a winning team, and you're trying to ruin our plans. Now our backs are up. We'll play a game here Tuesday night whether we have the arena or not."

Seymour laughed out loud. "That's impossible. You can't play hockey if you've got no ice."

"And we can't play road games unless we get some

gate receipts at home," Max said. He was furious. "So we'll play at home and we'll get some money somehow. And someday, Seymour, I'll be happy to stuff this contract down your throat."

Max and Marty walked to the door. Marty turned and said, "Old goats," once more.

That's when Myron Seymour lost his composure. He guessed that Eileen had told Max about the meeting. The thought that Eileen had sided with Max enraged him. And Max's threat to make him eat the contract enraged him even more.

"You get out!" he roared, grabbing Max by the arm. "A good thrashing would do you both some good."

Max stood firm. He brushed Seymour's arm aside. "A thrashing!" he said hotly. "And who's going to give it to me? Not you!"

"Just get out and stay out!"

"I'm leaving," Max said through clenched teeth, "but I won't be kicked out. If you think you can give me a thrashing, why not step out in the alley and try it?"

Seymour's face went scarlet. He had worked himself into a frenzy and issued fighting threats, only to have Max accept his challenge. Now he was in a bind. He couldn't back down now. But if the story ever got out that he'd lowered himself to brawling in an alley with a high-schooler, well, Mr. Gray would certainly be displeased.

"Come on outside, Myron," Max challenged. "Let's see how tough you really are. Come on, let's go."

"I'll give you something to remember me by, Mitchell," Seymour spat, rolling up his sleeves and striding toward the door, fists clenched.

"You must think you're the world heavyweight champ," snorted Marty. "I'm warning you mister. My brother doesn't fight often. But when he does, look out!"

In the alley, Seymour tried to take Max by surprise. He rushed the young hockey player, who was taking off his jacket and had his arm caught in a sleeve. Seymour was taller, older and heavier than Max and he'd been an amateur boxer with some skill at one time. He was out of shape but he was certain he could pummel Max into submission if he worked fast.

He shot out a left hand that caught Max on the side of the face. Then he followed up with a roundhouse right that knocked Max down. Max stayed down for a few seconds, until his head cleared and he was able to pull his arm free from his coat. He realized he'd underestimated Seymour's prowess as a boxer.

Max rose to his feet and covered up as Seymour, sensing victory, mercilessly pounded his head and shoulders. Max could feel anger begin to soar from within. He'd had enough of Seymour's fists. He pulled back, then ducked and waded in fast. He threw a series of punishing punches into Seymour's paunch, his soft spot. Max took another blow to the head, but now he could hear Seymour wheezing, a sign that his punches had taken a toll. Max drilled another hard right to the man's stomach and Seymour dropped his arms to cover his midsection. Max aimed another hard right to the head and it caught Seymour over his left eye. Blood spurted and ran down his cheek. Seymour staggered, his knees buckled and his mouth dropped open. He was glassy-eyed and gasping for air. Max knew the fight was over. Seymour was exhausted.

Still, the bigger man lunged in once more and took a wild swing that missed by a foot. He spun around, lost his balance and flopped into a snowbank.

"Was that a new dance step?" Marty taunted.

Max rubbed his hands and said to Marty, "That's it. Let's help him up." They dragged Seymour to his feet. Max said, "I didn't know you could fight like that, Seymour. If you were in any kind of shape, you probably could give me a beating. Listen, I hate fighting so let's shake hands and forget all about this."

But Seymour couldn't take a licking. He snarled some vile words at Max and Marty, turned and stumbled back to the door. He turned, wiped the blood off his cheek and called out, "I'll get you for this, Mitchell." The door slammed behind him.

Marty helped Max into his coat. "You showed him, brother. He won't fool around with you again."

"Maybe not with his fists," Max said, ruefully. "But he's got a mean temper, hasn't he? I'll bet even now he's plotting ways to get even." Max felt the bruise on his cheek. *Not so bad*, he thought.

"Well, let's go over to the rink," he said, tapping Marty lightly on the arm. "I've got to tell the boys the latest bad news. Don't make a big thing out of this fight. I try to set a good example by not getting involved in scrapping—on or off the ice."

Max didn't get into uniform and join his teammates on the ice. He called them together in the dressing room and told them what had happened. They listened in heavy silence. Of course, Marty hadn't been able to keep his mouth shut about the confrontation with Seymour.

Red Gadsby said bitterly, "Marty says you beat the heck out of Seymour. That's some consolation. I wish I'd seen it."

"He's a lot bigger than you," Chubby said. "And he was once a Golden Glove champ. Good going, Max. He had it coming. The bad news is that it looks like our season's over—after just one game."

"It's true, we can't play without ice," Kelly Jackson said glumly, tossing his stick into a corner. "I hate to hang up my skates now, especially after whipping the Beavers. I guess we were foolish to think we could buck the company and get away with it. I guess Myron Seymour is just too smart for us."

"No, he just thinks he is," snapped Max. "He may be smart enough to keep us off of the rink, but he can't keep us off the river. All that frozen ice, there's our new rink."

Red Gadsby whistled softly and began to smile. "Ah, the river," he said. "Where all of us learned how to skate." Other faces brightened.

"I never thought of the river as a rink," said Peewee Halloran. "You think we can pull it off?"

"Why not?" said Max. "The ice is a foot thick. We can clear the snow off the river, put up some boards, paint a few lines on the ice and we've got a rink. That's where the game was played around here a few years ago."

"Wait a minute," shouted Chubby Carlton. "League rules call for electric lights over the rink. I'm not tending goal while some guy holds a lantern over my net." Everybody laughed.

Max said with a grin, "Chubby, we won't be playing in the dark. And we'll follow league regulations. Now here's what I've got in mind..."

CHAPTER 10

ON OPEN ICE

Myron Seymour spent an unpleasant half-hour with the young woman he hoped would someday accept his engagement ring. It made perfect sense for Myron to be engaged to Eileen Gray—the boss's daughter. But Eileen quickly made it clear she was furious about the decision made by the rink committee.

"You're not being fair, Myron," she said hotly. "Those young men are doing their best to keep a hockey team together and you're doing everything in your power to stop them. What are you thinking? Depriving them of their rink is, in my opinion, despicable."

"But Eileen, dear..."

"Don't call me dear," she flashed. "You're on the committee and you could have prevented what happened."

"But I have only one vote. The others..."

"And I need only one guess to know how you

voted. You can sway that board of old codgers any way you want to. And you know it. If you told those men to jump in the lake, they'd do it, even if they fell out of their rocking chairs in the attempt."

"But, Eileen, I'm merely following your father's orders. He's the boss. I have no personal feelings toward any of the players."

"Then why play such mean tricks on them? As for Dad, I don't think he even knows what happened today. By the way, what happened to your eye? And your face is all bruised."

"Oh, I had a little accident. Fell on an icy patch. Why are you so interested in the hockey team, anyway?"

"It's just that Max and the boys have overcome so many obstacles to make hockey a success again..."

"Oh, I see. It's Max Mitchell you're interested in."

Eileen's voice turned icy. "And what have you got against Max?"

"Nothing. Nothing at all. It's just that he's a rebel, always tilting at windmills. He'll never amount to anything or even be accepted in our social circles."

"You have no right to judge him like that, no right to criticize my friends, Myron. And Max is a friend of mine. I like him."

"Oh, I know you like him, Eileen. You liked him enough to call him and tell him about the meeting of the arena committee, didn't you?" Seymour was angry, angry enough to say things he'd later regret. "You went behind my back and tried to ruin everything I planned. It's your fault that he and his brother... well, I wasn't going to tell you this... but they dragged me out to the alley and beat me up. One held my arms while the other pounded me. Too bad you've never seen the ugly side of Max Mitchell and his mouthy kid brother. There were no witnesses or I'd charge them with assault. And that's how I got these marks on my face."

If he was hoping for sympathy from Eileen, Myron didn't get it. "I don't believe a word of it," she scoffed. "You're bigger than Max and he's anything but a bully. If you were in a fight, I'll wager you started it. And if you beat Max up, I'll never speak to you again." She turned on her heel and left the room.

"But Eileen, let me explain..." The only answer was the slam of a distant door.

Myron Seymour had nowhere to go but home. Head down, he walked through the snow, thinking he'd just made a huge blunder. He had always imagined his courtship with Eileen would lead to marriage, and marriage would assist him in achieving his major goal—taking over the presidency of the company.

"Well, anyway," he told the snow-covered evergreens he passed, "she won't have a chance to see that Mitchell guy showing off on the hockey rink. There'll be no more hero worship for him. I've settled that. Someday she'll realize that I'm far the better man."

On the following day, Seymour got the shock of his life when he walked toward his office and glanced down toward the river. "What in the world is going on down there?" he muttered aloud.

A mob of men and boys were busily engaged in clearing the snow from the ice. Myron walked closer, stepping off a curb. A truck passed close by, throwing dirty snow all over his freshly pressed trousers. The truck lumbered toward the river and stopped. Teenagers swarmed the truck and immediately began unloading long sections of board fencing. Max and his teammates, along with many of their friends, were demonstrating that they hadn't lost yet. They were taking advantage of the early morning hours to make a rink of their own. Myron could hear them laughing and singing as they worked. Already, the ice was a huge blue-black rectangle against the surrounding snow banks.

"Hey, Myron, this is how enterprising kids run a hockey club when they have no money and no rink to play on," said a voice at Seymour's shoulder. Seymour turned and found himself looking into the cheerful grin of Johnny Gray.

"What are all the boards for?" he grumbled.

"The boys needed a fence for their rink," Johnny explained. "They were granted permission from the town council to relocate the fence from the old athletic track on the edge of town. "They're bringing it in by sections. Smart move, eh?"

"And whose idea was that?" Myron started to ask. "Oh, never mind, I can guess." He scowled, and then his face brightened. "Look! They've forgotten the lights," he snorted, breaking into a laugh. "They can't string lights over their rink without permission of the company. And the dummies are foolish to think they can charge admission. Everyone can watch them play for nothing."

"Looks as if they plan to carry on just the same," said Johnny, still smiling. "As for lights and gate receipts, there are the answers to both your questions, Myron." Johnny pointed to a nearby telephone pole. On it was tacked a poster that Seymour had overlooked. In bold letters, it proclaimed:

NORTHERN LEAGUE HOCKEY GAME

WOLVERINES VS. INDIANS

TUESDAY AT 3 P.M.

SILVER COLLECTION
HELP KEEP HOCKEY ALIVE IN INDIAN RIVER

Seymour was stunned. "But they can't play in the

afternoon," he roared.

"No law against it," returned Johnny. "They think they'll draw a good crowd from the guys on the night shift. And Max has talked the school principal into letting the kids out a little early. Promised him a hockey clinic in return."

"What about the players who work the day shift for the company? They're getting off early too?"

"Most of them have traded shifts with their pals. Come on, Myron, give them a little credit. Be a sport. Admit they've outsmarted you."

"I'll admit to nothing," Seymour choked.

"Have it your way," Johnny grinned. Then he gave Seymour an anxious look.

"My goodness, Myron, your face. It's all scratched up. Did my sister Eileen do that to you?" He slapped Seymour on the back. "I should have warned you she has a temper."

"No, of course not. I slipped on some ice and hit my head," Seymour grunted as he hurried off. Johnny Gray was still laughing when Seymour turned the corner.

CHAPTER 11

GETTING READY FOR THE WOLVERINES

The Hartley Wolverines were generally viewed as the elite of the Northern League. Not one team member had been born in Hartley and every player drew a paycheque because of his skill on skates. It was, in short, a team of ringers.

In the 1930s, Hartley was one of many towns that scoffed at the notion that a strictly amateur team could win more games than it lost. The best amateur players were lured to teams where money was plentiful. And Hartley had a couple of millionaires in town who loved the game and opened their wallets in order to get the best hockey players available.

This was the team Max and his mates were to meet in their first home game. It was a team to be respected and feared. In O'Grady and Madden, the Wolverines had two of the hardest-hitting defence-men in the league. They tried to outdo each other in hard hits and dirty tricks—most of them well out-side the rules.

The first line forwards were Mackenzie at centre, Gimpoli on right wing and Chakowski on the left side. All three were slick, fast skaters and tricky stick-handlers. All three were bad-tempered. The Wolverines boasted two other lines almost as good and a goalie named Legs Morton, who had been an All-Star in every league he'd played in.

Against them Max had Chubby Carlton, who compared favourably with any goalie in the North Country. Red Gadsby and Jim McEvoy packed a lot of muscle and were hard as nails on defence. Among his forwards, Max had Kelly Jackson who was developing fast. He was swift and strong and had perfected a blistering shot. Halloran, on left wing, was a lightweight who was quick and willing but lacked a scoring touch and experience. What's more, his ankle was still troubling him. Left wing was a weak spot. And there wasn't much depth on the bench.

On the weekend, Max had made a trip with Marty to an Indian reservation some distance away. Johnny Gray had told him of a native youngster who was the talk of the reserve because of his hockey skills. "I believe his name is Sammy Running Fox," Johnny had said. "Might be worth talking to him."

When Max and Marty arrived at the reservation,

the native boys were involved in a game of shinny on the river ice. Despite frigid temperatures, dozens of kids whooped it up as they chased after the puck. One immediately stood out. He was taller and more muscular than the other boys and he had a fluid skating stride, the hands of a natural goal scorer and he was a willing and accurate passer. Max noticed that, when the boy wanted to, he could easily keep the puck on his stick, darting this way and that, daring the others to take it away from him. None of them could. Then he laughed and relaxed, and gave up the puck to a group of smaller boys who raced away with it. Max had often played the same kind of keep-away game himself.

"Wow! He's something," Marty said in admiration. "He's got moves like Howie Morenz."

"As if you've seen Morenz, the greatest player in the National Hockey League."

"I may not have seen him play, but I've read all about him. And Dad says he's got the best moves."

"Okay, you're right. This kid Sammy does have good moves," Max agreed. "And he's a left hand shot. Let's go talk to him."

All chatter and movement on the river ceased when Max and Marty ventured onto the ice. The native boys stood in a group and stared at the interlopers with curiosity and a certain amount of suspicion.

Max approached the tall player and asked, "Are you Sammy Running Fox?" A big grin lit up the face in front of him.

"I'm Sammy," he replied. "But nobody calls me Running Fox. Not anymore. I'm Sammy Fox."

"You're quite a hockey player," Max told him. "My name is Max and this is my brother, Marty." The boys shook hands. "I play for a team in Indian River and we could use a fella like you. Would you like to join us?"

"Would I have to try out?"

"I don't think so. I can see you have great skills. I'm just not sure about your team play. We have a close-knit group and team play is really important to us."

Sammy said confidently, "I'm a good team player. I know I am. I just don't have a team to play on."

"How about joining ours?" Marty offered enthusiastically.

"All right. I'll ask my folks. I'm sure they'll be pleased." They own a car. They can drive me to games in Indian River. When they can't drive, I'll ride in on my horse.

"We can't pay you," Max added. "We're all amateurs."

"I play for fun," Sammy said. "Always have, probably always will. No hockey scouts ever come to a reservation looking for hockey players. You boys are the first." He laughed, showing beautiful teeth. "I've been waiting for you."

"There's another thing," Max added, hesitantly. "You may encounter some… resentment from some folks… on account of… well, you know. Is that going to be a problem?"

"My people are used to that," sighed Sammy. "My skin may be red… well, it's not really red but it's not like your skin. It's darker but it's also very thick. Most times, insults just bounce off." He laughed. "I know. You can find me a big pair of earmuffs to wear when I'm playing."

"It's a deal," Max said, chuckling. He shook Sammy's hand. The curious native youngsters standing nearby burst out in a round of applause.

"Before we go," Marty blurted out, "I have a question."

"What's that?" Sammy asked.

"Could I see inside a teepee some time, like when we come back next time? And do old men smoke peace pipes inside them?"

Sammy roared with laughter. "Well, next time I'll give you a grand tour of the reservation, Marty. And you'll see for yourself whether we smoke peace pipes or not. But you'll have to watch the sky every day for my signal telling you when to come."

"Signal? What signal?"

"Why, my smoke signal," Sammy said, winking at Max. "How else can I reach you—by telephone?"

Marty broke into a grin. He said to Max, "I like this

guy. He's got a sense of humour." Then he turned to Sammy, nodded at Max and half-whispered. "Unlike some people I know."

Outdoor game or not, the match against the Wolverines drew a huge crowd. The folks in Indian River had been more or less indifferent to the hockey team's battle with the company. They took it for granted the company was all-powerful and the Indians would never play a game. Now the citizens had seen that this young team was a resourceful, fighting squad. Max and his mates were creating quite a stir. It might be fun to go see them play. "Can I go, Ma? Can I watch the Indians playing on the river?" were questions asked by hundreds of small children living in almost every home in the community.

The activity on the river had highlighted the clash between the company and the team. Word of the rink committee's action in demanding exorbitant rent for the arena ice had spread and the townspeople were unanimously on the side of the players. Their ingenuity in providing a makeshift rink for themselves had further boosted their stock.

The fence from the abandoned athletic field had been laid out, then set in a narrow trench chopped into the ice. The base of the fence was then frozen into place.

"What a clever idea," Eileen Gray said to her brother. "Whose idea was that?"

"Give you one guess," he replied.

The sloping hillside provided a natural grandstand. Dressing rooms were located in a boathouse some distance away. A couple of wood-burning stoves had been installed and fired up among the canoes and paddles. Only Max and his buddies had known how much hard work had gone into the enterprise. With the help of loyal, energetic youngsters—who were, after all, the most avid hockey fans around—it had all been accomplished to everyone's satisfaction. And just in time for the arrival of the Wolverines.

When the Indians trooped toward their room in the boathouse, they were delighted to see a mass of people on the hillside, dressed warmly, huddled together and sitting on cushions and blankets. It resembled a Fourth of July picnic—but in winter and without the fireworks.

Suddenly a huge roar went up. People stood and pointed. In the distance, a horse and rider galloped over the snow along the river. The rider carried a hockey stick and he lifted it like a lance—a salute to the fans. The rider pulled to a stop beside the rink, then turned to speak with a group of fans. They pointed to the boathouse. The rider rode over, tethered his beautiful horse, and disappeared inside.

"Fellas, this is Sammy Fox, our new player," Max said, obviously pleased to see the newcomer. "Give him a good welcome."

The players greeted Sammy and shook his hand. Then Peewee Halloran took him aside. "Max told me you might make it and you'll probably start on left wing today. I really don't mind. I'm not jealous because the team comes first and I'm nursing a sore ankle. Have a great game. When I'm back in top shape, then I'll give you a battle for the position."

Sammy was touched. "Thank you, Peewee. By the way, is that your real name? We have many strange names on the reservation but no Peewees."

Halloran whispered in his ear. "My real name is Percival Wellington Halloran. But don't you dare tell anyone."

Max held court before the players went onto the ice. "We're still short a man or two, but we've got to put on a good show today," he reminded them. "We can't charge admission, and we're relying on the generosity of our fans to keep our team in business. We need new equipment and we need money for travel."

Just then, there was a commotion at the door and two more bodies pushed their way into the small room.

"Cripes, it's Steve Kennedy!" someone shouted. The players jumped up and rushed their former coach off his feet.

"How've you been, Steve?"

"We miss you, Coach."

Kennedy spoke softly. "I thought I'd come over from Chatsworth and see you boys in the big game," he said. "And I've brought you a surprise." He motioned behind him and a tall youth moved into the light.

"Hey, it's Barry Miller!" The room grew silent. Someone groaned softly.

"What are you doing back in town, Barry?" Max asked, warily.

Barry shifted back and forth. He was ill at ease. "Mr. Kennedy drove me here from Chatsworth. I'm moving back in with my folks. Mr. Kennedy has been a great influence on me ever since I left."

Steve took Max aside. "Barry is a dandy hockey player, Max. I know he used to mope and feel sorry for himself. Wasn't a good team player. But I've seen him mature over the past few months. He's a different person now. He's doing well in school. Goes to church every Sunday. He can help your club. I know he can. But, of course, it's your decision. If you think he'll disrupt things, then..."

Max looked Steve Kennedy in the eye. "Steve, you're the best hockey man I've ever known. And a great judge of character. Barry and I have had our differences, but if you say he has matured and can help us, tell him to go get his gear and get back here fast. We can use an extra player."

Steve laughed. "His gear's just outside the door," he said.

CHAPTER 12

PLAYING THE MIGHTY
WOLVERINES

The Wolverines, resplendent in their new yellow and black uniforms, were caustic in their comments about the outdoor rink on which they were forced to play. Outdoor hockey was a new experience for these pampered stars.

''What a bush league organization!" one of them was heard to complain during the warm-up.

"We'll give these kids a good thrashing and be back home in time to get a good night's sleep," said another, yawning. Overconfident, amused and scornful of the surroundings, the Wolverines were inclined to take it easy. Plenty of goals were bound to come against this group of youngsters.

But the first few minutes convinced them the game was not a farce. It would be anything but a walkover. Max and his boys displayed a swift, aggressive attack from the opening faceoff. The reputation of the mighty Wolverines obviously didn't mean a thing to these eager kids. Within five minutes, the crowded hillside was in an uproar.

One outstanding player can often make a team successful and Max was that player for the Indians. He was big and fast, a brilliant stickhandler and he possessed a powerful shot. Defensively, he had a deceptive poke check and a willingness to mix it with the strongest and toughest of the opposing forwards. Above all, he had hockey sense; the ability to anticipate what would happen next. He instinctively did the right thing at the right time. Without realizing it, the Indians had improved 100 percent because of his leadership, for he set an above-average standard.

During the warm-up, the two newcomers, Fox and Miller, seemed to catch the spirit instilled by Max. Each had size and skill and showed a determination to excel, to prove they belonged.

In the first five minutes, the Indians swept in on the Wolverine defence time and again, ripping into them with a bewildering series of swift passes and quick, accurate shots. Goalie Morton had to be at his best to keep them off the scoresheet.

The period was nearly over before the Wolverines began to realize that the afternoon could be a long one and that this crew of underdogs was going to be hard to beat. Late in the frame, after a verbal lambasting from their coach, the big guns of the visitors got down to business. Mackenzie, Gampoli and Chakowski put on a dazzling display of skating and stickhandling, one that carried them right into Chubby Carlton's goal crease. But he blocked everything they threw at him.

They buzzed around inside the Indians' zone like angry hornets, but they couldn't score—not with the puck carrier being skated into a corner or bowled over by a thumping bodycheck; not with slick passing plays being broken up at the last second; not with Carlton frantically batting or kicking out every chunk of rubber that flew his way.

The first period was scoreless.

The Indians were jubilant when they gathered in their dressing room in the boathouse. Meanwhile, a dozen kids with brooms swept the rink clean.

"We've got the town behind us at last," declared Chubby gleefully. "They know we've got a fighting team. Did you hear them cheering?"

"An awesome sound," yelled Red. "They cheered our every move."

"The Wolverines hated it—us showing them up. They'll be out to silence the crowd in the second period," stated Jim McEvoy.

Max turned to Sammy Fox and Barry Miller. "You fellas fit right in. You played well. I'm really pleased with you."

Smarting under the acid criticism of their coach,

the Wolverines went after goals in the second period. Whenever Peewee Halloran replaced Sammy Fox on left wing, the Wolverines' big line tested him and tied him up in knots. Gimpoli took a lead pass from Mackenzie, streaked around Halloran and went right in on goal. He laced a terrific shot to the corner. The puck flew over Chubby's outstretched glove and dropped into the net. First score for the visitors.

A few minutes later, Jim McEvoy drew a penalty when he sent Mackenzie flying over the boards and into a snowbank. When the Wolverine forward staggered to his feet, dazed and uncertain where he was, small boys ran over and threw snowballs at the visiting player until he scrambled back over the boards. Mackenzie recovered quickly and on the ensuing power play he drilled a long screened shot that caught the upper corner of the net. The Wolverines led two to nothing. The cheers from the crowd on the hillside became less frequent.

Max led a determined attack when his team was back at full strength. He made a solo rush the length of the rink, stickhandled brilliantly through the defence and rattled a hard shot off the goal post. Max swept in for the rebound, cradled the puck on his stick and wristed a shot toward Morton just as a defender wrapped an arm around his neck, pulling him down. Morton got his stick on the puck and deflected it away. Kelly Jackson was there and he took a wild shot at the net. Morton stopped that drive, too. Morton's goaltending was outstanding and the crowd applauded his great work.

Max snared another rebound moments later and had the open corner of the net facing him. Morton was scrambling back. Max never got the shot away because O'Grady swept his skates out from under him.

"Two minutes for tripping!" shouted the referee, pointing at O'Grady. O'Grady looked around. He was confused. "Where's the penalty box?" he said.

"Jump the boards over there," the referee motioned. "It's a park bench. You'll find it."

"This is some bush league operation," O'Grady complained. He leaped the boards in disgust and threw himself down on the park bench, which promptly toppled over backwards. O'Grady's feet flew skyward and his head and shoulders were buried in snow. The fans roared at his misfortune.

With the man advantage, Max and his mates set up their power play. The puck skimmed from man to man until one of them spotted an opening on the net. One shot flew at Morton, then another and a third. Morton was always there, diving, flopping and kicking. He turned back every attack. When O'Grady's penalty time expired, much of the steam had gone out of the Indians' attack. The second-liners came out for both teams. Max had to gamble that his subs would hold off the Wolverines for a minute or two.

A wind was sweeping along the river and dark clouds were forming in the sky. Light flakes of snow began to fall. But the vast crowd stayed put. The Wolverines had the wind at their backs. They stormed in on the home team and dazzled the spectators with a blend of skating, puck handling and passing. But before they could get their best shots away, Red and Jim flung their bodies savagely against their attackers and sent them sprawling in all directions.

Chubby Carlton performed acrobatics in the nets. But the onslaught was fierce and the end came when Thomas, a fleet second line forward, swept around a weary Red Gadsby and rifled a shot on goal. Chubby got his big glove on it—but for just a second. The disc spun to the ice. Thomas leaped in for it, but Gadsby recovered and knocked him flying into the end boards. MacInnis, a Wolverine winger, was trailing on the play and raced for the puck. He rapped it across the line for the third Wolverine goal. Max groaned. *Three goals down. Would the fans now disperse, saying they'd seen enough?*

The Indians held the visitors for the rest of the period. Chubby Carlton almost missed an easy shot because the wind and snow bothered him. He lifted his glove to wipe his face and got it down again just in time to deflect the puck over the boards.

The fans began turning up their coat collars. Some covered their faces with scarves. But they remained faithful. When the period ended, a roar of cheering swept down the hillside, shouts and cries of support that told the players, the fans were with them body and soul, win or lose.

CHAPTER 13

THE TIDE CHANGES

Eileen Gray and her brother Johnny leaned over the rail when the Indians skated out for the final period. Eileen beckoned to Max and he skated over. Her eyes were sparkling, her cheeks flushed with cold. Max thought she never looked prettier.

"Don't lose heart, Max," she said. "You can still win. If the Wolverines didn't have a miracle man in goal, the score would be tied."

"We'll find a way to beat him," Max said. "I promise you that. But Morton is darn good, isn't he?"

Johnny agreed. "It's too bad you have to face a world-class goalie for your first home game. But that's hockey, pal."

"We've still got a trick or two up our sleeves," Max said as he skated away.

With the change of ends, the Indians now had the wind at their backs. The Wolverines had difficulty skating into the little gusts that blew up and they lost some speed afoot. But with a three-goal lead, they had little to worry about.

Morton, their goaltender, had earned Max's respect. He'd taken everything the Indians had thrown at him and still looked as cool as ice cream. Max was ready to try something different.

Skating alongside Mackenzie, who controlled the puck, Max threw his stick out and swept the disc away. He tore after it and wheeled toward the Wolverines' zone. Suddenly, from centre ice, he sent a high, looping shot toward Morton. The wind helped the puck soar. A fine cloud of snow made it difficult to see. Morton caught a glimpse of the black object lazily floating toward him and he heard a shout of warning from his defence. He moved out, grabbed his stick tightly and tried to focus on the elusive rubber. It spun slowly out of the white haze, not ten feet away. Morton lunged for it in desperation. He was too late. The puck dropped over his shoulder and into the net.

For a moment, there was a stunned silence. Then the crowd realized what had happened. A great roar of delight swept along the hillside. The Indian River crowd, frantic with joy, pounded each other on the back and cheered the Indians' first goal on home ice.

Morton batted the puck out of his net. "What a fluke!" he growled in disgust. But he knew that it took expert marksmanship to loft a puck into the net from that distance. He also knew that Max had fired shrewdly, taking advantage of the wind and the snow and that he'd relaxed at the wrong time. He expected there to be one or two more surprises in store for him before the afternoon was over. He began to feel a little nervous.

"Long range shots," Max told his mates. "They seem to work."

The Wolverines, who had failed to take advantage of long distance sniping when the wind was with them, now cut loose in a series of rushes, savagely boring into Chubby Carlton. But snow was beginning to gather on the ice. The pace slowed and their passes went awry. The Indian forwards threw long, high shots into the Wolverine zone, shooting from outside the blue line, centre ice, from anywhere. The puck appeared suddenly out of the snow and bounced crazily around Morton, who no longer felt relaxed and confident. He began to fight the jitters.

After 12 minutes of play, Kelly Jackson shot wildly from a bad angle. The puck zipped by Morton's elbow before he could move to block it. Jackson threw his arms in the air and did a little dance on the ice. It was a big goal he'd scored. The Indians needed one more to tie the score.

The rest of the period was wild, perhaps the most amazing few minutes of hockey ever seen in the paper town. The wind increased, blowing into a storm and sheets of snow and hail were flung across the ice, stinging the cheeks of the players, the referee and the fans. Nobody left the hillside.

The Wolverine coach and his players let up a howl. "Call the game, ref! Conditions are atrocious. We win three to two."

The ref looked at his watch. "Only six minutes to play," he said. "It's as fair for one team as it is the other. I won't call the game. Play hockey!"

There was a wild battle for the puck in front of Chubby Carlton. He slid out and batted the puck over to Jim McEvoy. McEvoy raced away and heeding Max's advice, he lobbed a shot at Morton. It came from well outside the blue line. Morton juggled it; let it get away.

Max raced in like a greyhound. He grabbed the rebound and circled the net, O'Grady right behind him. Max came out but Morton had him figured. Max would try to wrap the puck around the goal post and slip it quickly inside. Morton slid over, hugging the post, anticipating the move. But Max surprised Morton. He pulled the puck away from the post, skating backwards now. He sidestepped a crushing check from Madden who went sprawling into the net, throwing Morton off balance. Max saw a tangle of arms and legs and a tiny opening at the net. He shot the puck through and leaped in the air when the goal judge, standing on the ice behind the net, waved a red flag. The score was tied!

The Wolverines sagged. They had shot their bolt. They had been on the attack almost steadily throughout the period and now they were tired and discouraged. They'd given up three goals and now they were ready to settle for a tie. They could always blame the elements for their third-period letdown. The Indians quickly took advantage of their sullen mood. They swarmed all over the visitors and bottled them up.

It was big Jim McEvoy who settled the issue. He flattened Mackenzie at centre ice and left him crawling along the ice on his hands and knees. McEvoy rifled a low shot from the blue line. Morton, nervous, harassed and upset, plunged across to stop it. But he was a split second too late. The puck clanged off the post and fell inside the net. The goal judge waved his flag again. The tie was broken. The crowd on the hillside went wild and the players on the ice leaped into the air and threw their sticks and gloves in all directions. For the first time in the game, the Indians held the lead, four goals to three.

"Stay calm. Stay focused," Max told his men. "Gadsby just took a penalty for slashing. Game's not over and now we're short-handed." He waved Sammy Fox over. "Remember that keep-away game you were playing when I first met you?"

"I remember."

"I want you to try it on the Wolverines. We've got two minutes to kill and we're all exhausted."

Sammy smiled. "I'm fresh. Just watch me."

The puck was dropped. Max won the draw and flipped the puck to Sammy. He started up ice, reversed direction and sped behind the Indians' goal. Surprised, the Wolverines just looked at him. Then they chased after him.

Sammy dashed into the corner, dragging the puck. Two Wolverines were right on him. But he eluded them both, still holding the puck. He started up ice again, darted left, then right and spun around in a circle. Now all the Wolverines were in pursuit. Time was running out and they wanted that puck. Sammy dared them to come and get it. They took up the challenge, but Sammy controlled the puck like a magician. With five opponents around him, he surprised everybody by skimming a short pass over to Max who was skating nearby. The Wolverines turned as one and chased after Max. When they closed in he threw the disc back to Sammy, who repeated his routine, which ended with all the Wolverines, except the goalie, chasing Sammy around the rink.

The whistle blew. The game was over.

The crowd on the hillside erupted. They swarmed down the slope, leaped over the boards and onto the ice. The Wolverines panicked, thinking they might be under attack, and ran for their dressing room. But they were in no danger. The fans wanted to show the Indians how much they cared. They lifted Max and Chubby onto their shoulders. They turned toward Sammy, and for a moment he thought of past treatments by white people. He thought he might have to flee. But they embraced him and put him on their shoulders too, saying they'd never seen such skill at stickhandling. The fans shouted their praise and delight.

Johnny Gray pounded Max on the back on the way to the dressing room. "All the world loves a winner," he cried over the hubbub. "A lot of these back-slappers are the same people who predicted you'd never play a game in this town."

Eileen Gray pushed past her brother. "Oh, Max, I'm so pleased for you. It was a marvelous comeback. I do hope the town will back you up now."

A number of celebrating fans came between them and Max was jostled toward the dressing room. Here he found his mates enjoying the attention and plaudits from a dozen fans who had wandered in. Chief among them, to his amazement, was Bob Barlow of the rink committee. He was red-faced and hoarse from cheering.

He pumped Max by the hand. "Why didn't you tell us you had such a grand team?" he asked. "Any team that can trim the Wolverines is a team to be proud of," the old man added.

"What are you getting at, Mr. Barlow?" Max asked.

"Now look here, son," he said, pulling Max down to a bench. "Let's get together. I know I haven't helped you, but I'm telling you now that Bob Barlow is on your side after today. I let Seymour persuade us to sign that rink contract because it made no sense to stir up trouble with the company just because a bunch of stubborn kids wanted to play hockey. It's different now. Maybe the company's not behind you, but the town is."

Max shrugged. "We'll see," he said. "But it's a little late coming around now, Mr. Barlow. You know we can't possibly sign Seymour's rink contract."

Before Barlow could reply, Marty burrowed his way through the players. "Max, they can't take away the fence enclosing the rink, can they?"

"What are you talking about, Marty? Of course, they can't."

"Well, they're going to do it. I just heard some men say it was coming down. Said something about it being company property."

"Oh, Lord," sighed Max. "What next?"

CHAPTER 14

BACK UNDER A ROOF

"We should auger a hole through the river ice and drop those company guys through it," Red Gadsby suggested. "Especially Myron Seymour. He'd feel right at home in the water because there's something fishy about everything he does."

"Yeah, he thinks he's a shark and we're the suckers," growled Kelly Jackson.

Through the door, they were watching the men taking down the fence surrounding the ice, the snow-covered surface on which the Indians had just defeated the Wolverines.

"It would have to be a big hole," snorted Marty. "Big enough to get his fat head through." The players muttered angrily in their dressing room. There was no doubt that Myron Seymour was behind the fence removal.

"The fence does belong to the company, boys," Bob Barlow agreed. "Afraid you can't do much about it."

"We put a lot of work into putting that rink up," snapped Max. "We're not going to give it up without a fight." He was tying the laces on his boots, ready to go out and confront the fence removers. His mates rose to go with him.

"Better forget it, fellows," Barlow suggested. "The rink contract drawn up by Seymour is flawed, as you know. I'm going to suggest we tear it up and write out a new one. At fair terms, I might add. So stop worrying."

"Can you swing that, Mr. Barlow?" Max asked eagerly.

"After the game you fellows played today. If I don't swing it, I may find myself kicked off the committee. Public opinion didn't give two hoots about you men yesterday, but there are any number of hoots on your side today."

Barlow was right. That night he succeeded in calling a special meeting of the committee to reconsider the rink contract. Myron Seymour, to his astonishment, found the other committee members allied solidly against him. He realized that nothing would be gained by bucking public opinion or the committee, so he meekly agreed to a new contract. It called for a reasonable share of the gate receipts and free practice time for the Indians.

"Mind you, they're still a troublesome bunch," Seymour couldn't resist reminding the committee.

"They had no right to take that fence from company property and put it on the river." He hesitated, lowering his gaze to make eye contact with each man on the committee. "Don't forget, men," he said in an ominous tone, "Mitchell brought in a redskin to play. That's just looking for trouble."

Nobody was listening. They were all talking about the game against the Wolverines. Seymour was furious when a committee member said, "Smart move by young Mitchell. I'd never have thought of that."

He jumped up and stormed from the room, a sour look on his face. Mr. Gray will hear about this, he promised himself.

Later that week, the team turned out for practice wearing brand new uniforms Max had purchased with the receipts from the Wolverine game. Max was surprised to notice Myron Seymour standing by the rink boards next to Johnny and Eileen Gray.

"The new uniforms look wonderful, Max," Eileen shouted across the ice. "A great choice of colours."

Max skated over to say hello. He was surprised when Seymour leaned forward, hand outstretched. "Let's bury the hatchet, Mitchell," he suggested. To Max, he looked about as sincere as a dentist saying, "This isn't going to hurt at all."

"Sure," Max agreed, shaking Seymour's hand. Inwardly he was wondering if he could trust the man. Perhaps he should try to peek up his sleeve; see what other surprises he was hiding up there.

Eileen was delighted when Seymour declared he was no longer opposing the team. "I'm a fan now—like everybody else in town," he told her, flashing her a smile.

"I'm so happy everything is cleared up," she told Max. "Your team will have clear sailing from now on."

"I hope so," remarked Max. But he wasn't sure there wouldn't be any further trials ahead. He suspected that Seymour's gesture of friendship was just that—a gesture. In fact, Myron Seymour was already making plans to ensure that the clear sailing Eileen had predicted would end up in the sinking of Max Mitchell's ship.

With two victories in as many starts, the Indians became the talk of the Northern League. They dropped a close game on the road to the Wolverines, but followed up with two wins at home against the Beavers and the Miners. They took another game from the last-place Miners but ran into trouble in Chatsworth when a flying puck knocked out Chubby Carlton and the Beavers scored three late goals on Tom Ardath, his substitute.

"I should have been there," snorted Marty. "I'm a better goalie than Ardath. And you know it, Max. You're afraid to play me because I'm your brother.

I'll bet Steve Kennedy would have put me in ahead of Ardath."

Max said he'd think about Marty's comments. "I want to be fair," he said. "It's difficult to put your own brother into a game and not be accused of playing favourites. Then again, it's unfair to you if I don't play you when you're at least as good as Ardath."

"You're the coach," Marty answered. "Maybe I'm the only one who thinks I'm better than Ardath. But I know one thing. I have a better attitude than he does. He's going to give you a big headache. Wait and see."

The Wolverines shot to the top of the league standings and when they returned to Indian River, they were determined to avenge the loss they'd suffered on the outdoor ice and the whole town turned out to root for the home team.

It was a bitter battle, but by this stage of the season the Indians had gained a lot of experience. The team was vastly improved over the eager but amateurish squad that had depended on guile and a snowstorm to give them a slim victory over the Wolverines in the home opener. Inspired by the cheers of the townspeople the Indians skated brilliantly. Sammy Fox's dazzling display of stickhandling and Barry Miller's rink-length dash that resulted in a goal were the highlights. The final score was Indian River 1, Wolverines 0.

As satisfying as the victory was, Max had a problem to deal with after the game. Backup goaltender Tom Ardath approached him with a surprise ultimatum.

"My folks don't want me playing on the same team with an Indian. They say it's a disgrace."

"Is that so?" Max answered hotly. "What's wrong with Sammy Fox?"

"He's an Indian, not one of us. He's different, is all. My folks think he should stay on the reserve where he belongs."

"And what do you think, Tom? You're old enough to make up your own mind."

Tom fidgeted and said, "What can I do, Max? My folks don't want me playing with him."

"Then your folks are bigoted, Tom. And it looks like you are too. Are you trying to tell me you'll quit the team if I keep Sammy?"

"Yes, I guess I am. But I think you should keep me and get rid of him. Everybody knows you don't have another decent backup goalie and…"

"I'm really sorry you feel this way, Tom. But there's no way I'm dropping Sammy Fox. You're off the club."

"If you kick me off the team, you'll be sorry. I just told you. You have no backup."

Max laughed. "Tom, I didn't kick you off. You quit! That's fine with me." He jabbed his finger at the other boy's chest. "I'm not having a bigot on my team. I have the perfect backup goalie ready and waiting: my brother Marty. He doesn't mind if the skin of a teammate is red, black or yellow. Neither do any of the other guys. Now turn in your jersey and take a hike."

The victory over the Hartley Wolverines kept the Indians in the hunt for the league title. On the final weekend they were neck and neck with the Wolverines for the championship. The title would be decided on the result of the final game played on the Wolverines' ice. By then Marty Mitchell had joined the club and was thrilled to be a part of all the excitement.

The Northern League championship! If the Indians won, as a junior team, they would be invited to compete for the national junior title to be played in the big arena in Boston. Two other clubs, the Cubs and the Supremes were in the running. And if the Wolverines won the big game, they would compete for the national senior crown.

The fact that the Indians had bested the Wolverines twice, rankled the fans in Hartley. And surprised some others, like Pete Clarke, longtime hockey writer for one of the big city dailies.

What's happened to the Hartley Wolverines? Billed as one of the slickest hockey clubs in amateur hockey and shoo-ins for the Northern League title, it appears the club may have difficulty getting out of their own league. Twice a squad of unknown youngsters from a little-known mill town has knocked them off. So the Wolverines can't be so hot, after all.

This Indian River club, with Max Mitchell, a teenage playing coach leading the way, won't draw flies if it wins tomorrow and moves on to Boston for the nationals. Why? Because it hasn't any stars. The kids are all hometown boys. Unknowns. Hicks from Hicksville. Hockey fans don't want that sort of colourless outfit in the finals.

Red Gadsby was particularly hot when he read Clarke's article. He was all for spreading doggy-doo on the article and sending it to Clarke by mail, suggesting he eat it for lunch.

"That's disgusting," said Chubby, who had once consumed calves' brains and pronounced them "a delicacy," grossing out his teammates.

"So he thinks because none of us are famous, we can't be any good," Red snorted. "I'd like nothing better than to go to Boston and win that junior title. How good can the Cubs and the Supremes be?"

"Plenty good, I'll bet," said Chubby Carlton. "But if we can do well against senior teams, we should be able to beat top junior clubs. We do that and we'll make Clarke eat his words."

"Forget Clarke," suggested Max. "We've got more important things to think about—like beating the Wolverines. We'll worry about winning in Boston when we get there."

When the boys piled on board the train bound for Hartley, two extra Pullman cars were added to accommodate the mob of fans eager to accompany them. Max couldn't help but compare the journey with their first out-of-town trip to Chatsworth. They had shivered in a boxcar and reached their destination half-frozen, hungry, tired and discouraged. And it had been dangerous. Now they travelled in a Pullman with their skates, sticks and other equipment locked in a box in the baggage car. In Chatsworth, they'd had no supporters; now there were a few hundred along to cheer them on. Even Myron Seymour was among the faithful.

"The guy must be becoming somewhat human," he said to himself. "Next thing you know I'll be calling him likeable."

CHAPTER 15
A CRISIS IN HARTLEY

They reached Hartley by mid-afternoon. The fans raced from the train and made a mad dash to the arena to buy whatever tickets were still available. Max was surprised to see Eileen and Johnny Gray at the station.

"We drove up," Johnny explained. "Couldn't get tickets for the train. Dad loaned us his fancy car. It's big and heavy and holds the road like nothing else on four wheels."

The team went to a hotel to rest up for a few hours, four to a room. Max kicked off his shoes and told his roommates—Red, Chubby and Jim—to get the game off their minds. "Take a little nap. Try to relax."

Then the door to their room flew open and Peewee Halloran popped through the door. He looked like he'd been outrunning a ghost. "Hey, Max!" he yelled. "What happened to the box?"

"What box?"

"The box with all our equipment in it."

Max leaped off the bed. "I gave the baggage check to the porter downstairs and told him to see that the box was delivered to our dressing room at the arena."

"But it didn't get there," howled Peewee. "It's gone! The baggage master said it wasn't unloaded from the train. The game starts in less than two hours and we haven't got a skate, a stick..."

Max reached the telephone in one bound. Within minutes the room was in an uproar. Team supporters came raging in, bursting with the news. Max called the station and reached the baggage master and the station agent. He called the porter and the rink manager. Everyone was apologetic but helpless. No one knew anything about the missing equipment box.

"Was it ever loaded onto the train in Indian River?" he asked his mates.

"Yes, I saw it go aboard," someone said.

"We can borrow equipment," Kelly Jackson said. "But you know what it'll be like. Skates won't fit; sticks won't feel right. This is a disaster."

The telephone rang and Max snatched it up. "Station master speaking, Mr. Mitchell. About that box. I'm awfully sorry, I don't know how it happened, but..."

"Where is it?" Max shouted into the mouthpiece.

"Apparently it was unloaded at a town named

Fensom, about 12 miles up the line. Our man there says it was checked through to Fensom and he has the baggage check to prove it."

"Yikes! How soon can we get it back? When's the next train?"

"There is no train, Mr. Mitchell. Not until tomorrow." Max hung up. He was fuming. He looked at his watch. Ten minutes had elapsed since he'd received the shocking news. He told his players to get over to the rink.

"Borrow some equipment from the Wolverines or the local high-school team. Stall as long as you can. The rink is sold out and they won't want to cancel. They'll co-operate. I'll be back as soon as I can." He grabbed his jacket and dashed out the door.

Snow and slush flew in all directions as the powerful car drove straight up the middle of the road leading to Fensom. Johnny Gray was at the wheel with Eileen beside him. Max Mitchell occupied the back seat.

"Be careful, Johnny, you're almost up to 50 miles per hour," Eileen cautioned.

"Eileen, it's almost game time and we're not even in Fensom yet," Johnny replied, twisting the wheel to avoid a patch of snow in the road.

"There are street lights ahead. It must be Fenson," Max shouted from the back seat.

In Fensom, they had no trouble locating the train station perched in the centre of town. The baggage master, sitting on a large wooden box, a lantern next to him, was waiting for them.

"My gosh, I didn't know the box was so big," Max said. "It'll never fit in the trunk of your car."

"You're right," said Johnny. "Maybe we can tie it to the roof."

"Impossible. It's too heavy. There's only one answer," exclaimed Max.

When they drove off, the baggage master was laughing. He'd never seen three people empty a box so fast. Skates and sticks and shin pads and gloves were hurled into the back of the car. Several sticks stuck out an open window. Eileen carried a first aid kit and a box of hockey tape on her lap. She held up a jock strap and Max snatched if from her and tossed it in the back seat. Max hurled himself on top of all the equipment in the back seat and lay down on a pair of goalie pads. "Take off, Johnny!" he hollered.

"Someone will come back for the box tomorrow," Johnny called to the station master as he pulled away, his rear tires spraying the poor man with slush.

They zoomed back down the road to Hartley, directly into the face of a bitter wind.

"You better open your window, Eileen. The air in here is pretty foul."

"Whew!" Eileen laughed, holding her nose. "Perhaps I should pour some perfume over this smelly gear."

Max smiled. "Well, it might make for a nice change. But I doubt the players would feel right if their gear smelled like gardenias."

Johnny had trouble keeping the car on the road as snow began to fall. Twice he had to swerve to avoid slamming into snowbanks. Once he hit the brakes to avoid a deer crossing the road and the heavy car swung almost completely around.

Max looked at his watch. Fifteen minutes past eight. The game would be well underway by now.

The hazardous ride seemed to go on forever, but it was only 8:30 when the arched roof of the Hartley arena marked their destination.

The referee was sympathetic to the Indians' plight and waited until well after the eight o'clock start time to call the teams to centre ice. But the Hartley fans, annoyed at the delay, had set up a riotous chant of annoyance at the delay. "Play hockey! Play hockey! Play hockey!" they shouted. After all, the visitors had been provided with enough equipment, hadn't they? All but the backup goalie. Nobody had been able to find a second set of pads for Marty. Skates and sticks and other gear came from one of the school teams in town. So what if the borrowed gear didn't fit? Beggars can't be choosers.

"Come on, ref! Start the game!" a fan bellowed.

The Indians looked uncomfortable in their ill-fitting equipment. The fans who came to cheer them on turned gloomy at the sight of their shabby appearance. Chubby Carlton made an attempt to stall for a little more time when he pulled the untied skatelace trick and drew a razzing from the crowd.

Finally the referee threw down the puck and the crowd roared. The game was underway.

The Indians immediately put up a stubborn defence against the smooth, hard-hitting Wolverines.

Before a home crowd, with the odds in their favour, and the league title in sight, the flashy forward line of Mackenzie, Gimpoli and Chakowski played with dash and fire. With an abundance of speed, they zipped past their Indian River counterparts and swooped in on the defence like hunting dogs after a fox. But there the comparison ended.

They entered a hornet's nest in front of the Indian River goal. Red Gadsby and Jim McEvoy savagely defended Chubby Carlton and the goal cage behind him. A pair of husky young giants, the two rearguards laid into the attackers with the desperation of men on a mighty mission. Despite the strange skates that bothered their feet, they hit that fast forward line hard and often. They shook them up, hurled them back and made them think twice about coming back for more.

The crowd screamed with excitement and groaned in despair as scoring plays were broken up, as shot after shot flew toward the net where Chubby Carlton leaped in front of each and every one of them.

Midway through the first period, the Wolverines caught a break. Sammy Fox, stickhandling expertly out of his own zone, watched in dismay as the puck hit a rough spot in the ice and bounced away. Mackenzie was there to trap it. He threw a quick pass over to Gimpoli and the wrist shot that followed sent the puck flying over Chubby Carlton's glove. The Wolverines had scored first.

"It's all right. What's one goal?" Red Gadsby roared. "Don't let it worry you."

But even Gadsby, despite his brave words, was concerned. He knew the Indians couldn't play defensive hockey all night. They had to score and so far they hadn't taken a shot on Morton, the idle Hartley goaltender. Most of the equipment they'd borrowed was far too small. They couldn't move freely in tight-fitting skates and pants.

It was then that Chubby Carlton, crouching in goal, heard a familiar voice from behind the wire fence.

"Chubby! The equipment's here. It's in the dressing room."

The goalie shot a glance over his shoulder. Max was loaded down with a bundle of sticks, jerseys and skates.

"Hallelujah!" crowed Chubby, turning just in time to take a whistling shot off his chest. "Ooof," he groaned. He threw his arms in the air and dropped to the ice. It looked as if a heavy beam had fallen from the roof and flattened him. He lay on his back motionless. The crowd fell silent, stunned by the sight. Chubby's eyes were closed.

His teammates rushed over and kneeled over him.

"It looks bad, really bad," Jim McEvoy told the referee, shaking his head sadly, his eyes wide with concern. "Quick! Let's get him into the dressing room."

His teammates carried Chubby off the ice on a stretcher.

"Have you got a team doctor?" the referee asked.

"We sure have," said McEvoy. "Someone run and get Dr. Small."

Peewee nudged Marty and whispered, "Hey, ain't Doc Small a vet?"

"Ssh!" Marty hushed him. "The ref doesn't know that."

Inside the dressing room, Chubby snapped open his eyes and roared with laughter. The players whooped with delight. Max Mitchell was pulling off his street clothes and donning his hockey gear. "Let's go, fellows," he shouted. "Someone bolt the door!" Jerseys and socks flew through the air.

There was a knock on the door. The players fell silent. The referee could be heard asking about Chubby's welfare.

"Dr. Small is with him and he's coming around," Red Gadsby shouted out. "Give him another few minutes." He nodded at Chubby who groaned loudly, sounding like a bear with a paw in a trap.

"Okay. But no longer."

"Sure, ref. You're a considerate man," said Red, rolling his eyes.

Chubby snickered. "I'll bet the Wolverines will be sore when they find out I was pulling an act."

"Let 'em be sore," grunted Red. "I'm sore too— from knocking them down every few seconds."

"Before we go out there," Max said quietly as he finished lacing his skates. "I want you all to know how proud I am that you held them to one goal. Great work, men."

Ten minutes after Chubby's near fatal "injury," the Indians were back on the ice. The Hartley fans were shocked by the transformation. This was a new team, with new uniforms and sharp skates. They swarmed onto the ice as fresh and eager as if the game had just begun.

The Wolverines—so brash and confident in the opening minutes—now appeared confused. They were caught napping when Max cut loose right from the faceoff and led an attack into the enemy zone. He drilled a shot—the first of the game for the Indians—at Morton in goal. The rubber bounced off the netminder's shoulder and skimmed over the cross bar. Morton winced and grabbed his shoulder. Geez, he grimaced, that kid can shoot.

Morton's mates, meanwhile, couldn't get back into that relentless, conquering stride that had worked so well for them earlier. They now found themselves playing much of the game behind their own blue line where, until now, the ice had barely been marked by skates.

Max was in top form. He outwitted Mackenzie at centre, knocked him sprawling twice and laid perfect passes to his wings. When he rested, Sammy Fox and Barry Miller teamed up on some exciting rushes. One of Miller's shots clanged off the goal post.

With two minutes left in the period, Max worked his way in close, evading the defence with a neat shift and whipped the puck toward the corner of the net. Morton stopped it and flung it aside. Gimpoli tried to pick it up, but Kelly Jackson raced in, hooked the puck away and swung in behind the net. Morton slid across and placed his skate firmly against the post, hoping to prevent a wrap around goal.

But Kelly crossed him up, sliding the puck out to Max in the slot. Max was charged by both O'Grady and Madden and was swept off his feet. But not before he slipped the disc over to Peewee Halloran who flipped an ankle-high shot through a tangle of legs and sticks. The puck caromed off Morton's right leg and flopped into the net.

Goal! Indian River fans rejoiced, making their presence felt with a deafening roar.

On the ice, Peewee Halloran smiled slyly at Morton. "We'll be back this way for another little visit real soon," he promised. Morton snarled a reply, then turned away and fished the puck out of the net.

When the period ended, the crowd realized they were watching a championship tilt after all. The early advantage held by the Wolverines had disappeared. The home team would have to regroup and fight back.

All through the second period the battle raged without letting up. The play shifted from one end to the other with bewildering speed. Each goalie had close calls that brought the crowd to its feet, howling hysterically.

It had been a cleanly played game up to this point with each team fearful of the other's power play. The penalty box remained empty and the score remained tied at one.

During the second intermission, Max cautioned his players. "Hartley has spent a lot of money on the Wolverines," he said. "The fans want something in return. There are some big egos in the other room. They are frustrated and angry and they'll likely start roughing us up in the final period."

"Let 'em try," growled Red Gadsby. "I'll hand out a receipt for every slash or cross-check they lay on me."

Max shook his head. "No, Red. You've got to stay in there and take it. Let the ref hand out the receipts. No penalties. I mean it. Stay cool."

The teams began the third period and Max found out he'd guessed right. The play became much rougher. Nothing serious at first. Heftier body-checking, a sly slash when the referee had his back turned. Mackenzie took a run at Max and tripped him, punching him hard in the face when he fell. No penalty. The Wolverines were crafty and mean. They were trying to provoke the visitors into retaliating. Max got up, shaking his head. He glared at Mackenzie who scooted away. "I'll see you later," he called after him.

Midway through the period, with the score still tied, Barry Miller was barreling down the wing when he collided with an opposing player. Max saw the butt end of a stick slip out and catch Miller in the ribs. It was a dirty blow. Miller stopped and spun around. He raised his stick high and then he remembered Max's edict—no penalties. He turned his back and skated away.

The crowd booed Miller. There were cries of

"Yellow!"

"That's hard to take," Max said to Marty, who occupied the end of the bench. "Miller has turned out to be a good kid, even better than Coach Kennedy predicted."

Moments later, Miller took a hard pass from Sammy Fox and raced over the blue line. Big Madden had him lined up and launched into a check that, had it landed, would have flattened Miller. But Miller stepped aside, and Madden crashed knees-first into the boards. Frustrated, the lumbering defenceman turned and lashed out with his stick, sending Miller sliding along the ice.

"Two minutes for tripping!" bawled the referee.

"There's our break!" Max shouted as he leaped over the boards. "Let's make the most of it."

With the man advantage, the Indians swept into the Wolverines' zone. Morton stopped three or four hard shots with his glove, stick and chest. Max moved right in, pulled Morton aside and flipped the puck high—too high. The disc hit the crossbar and fell into Morton's crease. He slapped it hard with his goal stick and sent it skimming toward centre ice. Suddenly, Mackenzie snapped it up and raced away—on a breakaway. He had only Chubby to beat. He weaved in, faked a shot. Chubby didn't move. Desperately, Mackenzie whipped the puck high and Chubby calmly batted it to the corner where Kelly

Jackson was waiting.

Jackson grabbed the puck and circled the net, gathering speed. He was over his own blue line and breaking for the enemy goal before the Wolverines could pull themselves together. Mackenzie had stopped to tell Chubby what he thought of him and they pushed at one another. Mackenzie's tantrum left him out of the play.

Max and Peewee skated hard to keep up to Kelly, who faked a pass and moved around O'Grady. Then he sent a crisp pass onto Max's outstretched stick— right on the tape. From 20 feet, Max faked a shot to the upper corner, Morton leaped up to stop it, but the shot never came. Max calmly slapped the puck into the open corner of the net.

Indian River 2; Hartley 1.

Max Mitchell's goal was the biggest in the history of hockey in Indian River.

In the few minutes that remained, the Wolverines lost their composure. They tried to roughhouse their way toward Chubby's net and the sheer savagery of their attack earned them two costly penalties. In the stands, the shocked Hartley crowd watched with growing disgust as their expensive, imported players resorted to bush league tactics against a much younger and much less experienced team. Some began to boo.

With 15 seconds to play, Mackenzie made a final

dash down the ice, desperate to score the tying goal. He flew over centre ice and wound up for a hard shot on goal. He looked down at the puck—and whammo! Max came from the side and stepped into him with a clean bodycheck. Mackenzie flew high in the air, and then crashed to the ice, gasping for breath. Max took a moment to lean over and say in his ear, "I told you I'd see you later."

The seconds ticked away. Max smiled when he heard the bell.

Game over. Indian River wins.

Indian River fans stormed onto the ice, threw hats into the air, staged an impromptu march around the rink and carried some of the tired players to their dressing room. Even the Hartley fans were on their feet for a standing ovation.

Johnny Gray, flushed with the excitement of the moment, told Max while pounding him on the back, "Oh, boy, if my dad would only let me play."

"Work on him, Johnny," Max replied. "You've practiced with us all season. Your name is on our list. Stand up to the old man."

CHAPTER 16

A MYSTERIOUS DONATION

The train back to Indian River left at midnight. That gave the fans of the winning team some time to celebrate the great victory. Hartley residents claimed they'd never heard such a ruckus along the main street.

Max Mitchell had escaped all the backslapping and had found Eileen waiting outside the dressing room.

"Let's get a quick bite to eat," he proposed. "I'm starving."

She slipped her hand under his arm and they fought their way through the crowd. Many Indian River fans were collecting wagers they'd made on the game. Myron Seymour was among them. Seymour caught sight of Max and Eileen, grimaced and turned away. Eileen was chattering excitedly and hadn't noticed Seymour. They crossed the street and found a restaurant.

They talked about the wild ride they'd had to

Fensom and back. They laughed at how Johnny had sprayed the station master with snow and slush.

"He took quite a soaking, poor guy. And he was only doing us a favour. And he did us a bigger favour by convincing a friend with a truck to deliver the box to our dressing room."

"But how did the box get there in the first place?" Eileen wanted to know.

"Beats me," answered Max. "I think somebody changed the label on the box. There's been some dirty work somewhere."

"You mean someone deliberately tried to ruin your chances of winning?"

"Absolutely. The Hartley fans wagered a lot of money on the game tonight. I don't know much about the gambling, but someone told me the odds shot up just before game time. That's suspicious because we were an even money bet."

Eileen sipped her coffee. "I find it hard to believe people take hockey so seriously. And wager money on it. But I'm thrilled you and the team will be going to Boston for the national title. I hope Dad will let Johnny and me go on the trip."

"It's going to be an expensive proposition," Max sighed. "A long trip for a couple of series against the Cubs and the Supremes. Railways fares, meals, hotel bills—I don't know how we're going to pay for it."

A shadow crossed their table and Max looked up to see a stranger at his elbow.

"Max Mitchell?"

"Yes."

A heavyset man wearing a blue trench coat and a brown hat said quietly, "Could I see you for a moment?" He turned to Eileen, tipped his hat and said, "Sorry, ma'am."

Max excused himself and left the booth. The stranger drew him aside and without a word, handed Max a sealed envelope.

"What's this?" Max asked the stranger.

The man smiled. "This is just a little donation from me to your team. But don't say anything about it to anyone, not even your girlfriend over there. Got it?"

"Why, sure, but—"

"No buts. Just promise me you won't say anything about it."

"Of course I'll promise. And thank you. But why not tell me who you are?"

The stranger shook his head, turned away and hurriedly left the restaurant.

Max stood there, watching the fellow disappear through the door. This was certainly the oddest fan he'd ever encountered.

He went back to the booth and true to his promise, said nothing to Eileen about the gift.

"Just a big fan," he told her. "Now," he said, looking into her beautiful eyes, "what were we talking about?"

The next morning Max remembered the unusual meeting and pulled the envelope from his pocket. Inside were four crisp new 50-dollar bills. Max noticed that all four bills had a small brown stain on one corner.

"Wow! That's more than I expected," he exclaimed. "This solves a lot of our problems with expenses."

Later in the morning, Myron Seymour left a message for Max at school and invited him to a meeting at the mill. When Max arrived during his lunch break, Seymour took him to the treasurer's office where he ordered the treasurer to make up a cheque for 50 dollars—to help the team get to Boston and back. The treasurer nodded. "I'll have to get Mr. Gray to sign this," he said. "Myron, come with me. Wait here, son. We'll be right back."

Max was alone in the room for several minutes. He began to think that Seymour wasn't such a bad fellow, after all. When the men returned, there were handshakes all around and he pocketed the donation.

He rushed down to the bank and deposited the company cheque for 50 dollars, plus the four 50-dollar bills the stranger had given him and a few other small donations he'd received the night before. On the street, he ran into Bob Barlow of the rink committee.

"You raised over three hundred dollars!" Barlow exclaimed in amazement. "That's great, Max."

"I had a little luck, Mr. Barlow." But he failed to mention the large donation from the stranger in the restaurant.

That evening the hockey club held a meeting. It was well attended, in marked contrast to the first meeting of the season, when Max and his mates had been obliged to fight for the opportunity to play hockey at all.

Barlow made a windy speech, acting as if the Indians were his own special property and it was all his idea to revive hockey in Indian River. He announced that ample funds had been raised to see the team off to Boston where he had no doubt a championship awaited them. What's more, he said, President Gray of the mill had generously given time off to the players on the team employed by his company. The high-school principal had followed suit.

Johnny Gray told Max, "I think my dad is coming around. Of course, you ticked him off when you went ahead and organized a team against his wishes. But he's big enough to admit he was wrong. And I've got a sneaking idea that he may even let me play. If you need me, that is."

"We sure need you, Johnny. It's a good thing you've been skating with us almost every day. You can play on my left wing and I'll put Peewee on the second line."

"I hope to be with you on the train tomorrow night," said Johnny. "And if you hear from Dad tomorrow, you'll know he's jumped on the hockey bandwagon."

Max did hear from President Gray the following day. There was a summons to come to his office. "Yahoo," thought Max, "the old boy has finally come around." After school, he rushed over to the company and was whistling as he strode down the corridor.

Mr. Gray was sitting behind a huge, glass-topped desk. Instantly, from the coldness of the man's expression, Max knew he was in for trouble.

Next to Gray were the mill manager and the company cashier. A representative of the local bank was also in attendance. All looked grim and uncomfortable.

"I have called you here, Mitchell," said Gray, "to investigate the matter of a bank deposit you made yesterday at noon hour."

"Yes, sir, I sure did. Made a deposit for the hockey club."

"How much was the deposit, Mr. Mitchell?"

"A little over 300 dollars, sir, including the amount you donated."

"And how did you raise the money?"

"Some people gave me various amounts. Let's see, I have a list here."

He produced a notebook in which he had listed the donations including the one from the mill. Gray looked it over.

"This amounts to a little more than a hundred dollars. How about the rest of it?"

Max hesitated, and then said, "There was another donation of 200 dollars, sir."

"Was there? And who donated that?"

Max stammered. "Why, I'm not at liberty to tell, sir. And to tell the truth, I really don't know."

President Gray's lips formed a tight line. "You don't know? Then what were the denominations of the bills?"

"Four fifties, sir."

Gray swung around and confronted the bank representative.

"Do you have the four 50-dollar bills Mitchell deposited yesterday?"

"I do, Mr. Gray. We don't get many teenagers depositing 50-dollar bills." He reached in his pocket and produced the bills.

"Sir, these are the bills you asked about. You'll see each one has a small brown stain in one corner."

"Mitchell, are those the bills you put in the bank?"

"Don't know, sir. I guess so. If the banker says they are. What's the problem? They're not counterfeit, are they?"

Mr. Gray ignored the question.

"Were you in the treasurer's office yesterday morning where he left you alone for several minutes?"

"Yes, he went to your office to get a cheque signed."

"Our dilemma is this, Mr. Mitchell, Our treasurer discovered last night that four 50-dollar bills had been taken from his cash box. It has been proved that those four bills were the ones you deposited yesterday after you left this building."

The treasurer took a step forward. "Mr. Mitchell," he said, "I accidentally spilled some coffee when I was counting money from the cash box a couple of days ago. Some of the coffee stained the corners of those fifties. That's how we know they're the same ones you deposited."

Max was astonished.

"That's impossible!" he exclaimed. "Are you accusing me of stealing those bills from your cash box? I got those bills from a man in Hartley—after the hockey game."

"Who gave them to you?"

Even as he spoke, Max knew his story didn't sound plausible.

"It was a complete stranger, a man I'd never

seen before. Said he wanted to make a donation to the team..."

"And he didn't give his name?"

"No, sir. He said he wanted it kept quiet. Told me not to tell anyone about the gift."

"And I suppose you were all alone when this happened?"

"No, I wasn't alone." Then Max blushed. He couldn't drag Eileen into this. Max faltered. Besides, she hadn't seen the stranger give Max the envelope.

"Well, I was alone. You'll just have to take my word for it."

"Which I refuse to do," snapped Gray. "The only thing I can say in your defence is that you weren't about to use this money for your personal use. There's no doubt the money was taken from our premises and you had the perfect opportunity to pilfer it. It confirms my belief that hockey in this community leads to all kinds of bad behaviour, including petty theft."

"Mr. Gray, I'm no thief!" Max said, his voice rising sharply in anger.

"We can't prove that you are—not absolutely," said Gray. "That's why I won't press charges. I'll let the money go as a donation to the team. It'll be our final donation—ever. What's more, I don't want to see you in the building ever again and I don't want you associating with either of my children. You hear me, Mr. Mitchell?"

"I hear you, sir," Max said in whisper.

"You may leave now."

CHAPTER 17

GOALS TO COUNT

The supreme test of a small town junior club accustomed to playing on small natural ice surfaces is to take the measure of a crack, hard-hitting squad whose playground is the immense artificial ice surface of a big city arena. In the 1930s, small town teams fortunate enough to play championship games in cities like Toronto, Montreal and Boston were often mesmerized by the huge crowds and the bright lights in the mammoth arenas. For many players, it was a nerve-wracking experience.

For that reason, few were surprised when the Indians ran into trouble when they met the Boston Cubs in the semi-finals for the national title. In the opener of their two game series, with total goals to count, the Indians were shutout three to nothing. To the fans who made the long journey from Indian River to the big city, the result was a major disaster.

They were blunt in their post-game comments.

"The Indians played like they had weights on their skates," said Doc Small. "I've got sick kittens in my office who show more fight than those fellows."

Bob Barlow, who no longer called the Indians "my boys," said he predicted they were headed for a fall. "They were outclassed from the beginning. All hope for a championship is now gone."

Myron Seymour had profited handsomely by the Indians' defeat. He'd been smart enough to bet on the Cubs. "I knew that punk Mitchell would come apart under pressure," he crowed to several fans. "He folded like an old ironing board."

Meanwhile, the players were worried about Max. He'd been slow and listless. He was never a factor in the game. Where was his old fire and dash? And his shooting was atrocious. Twice he'd missed an open net when Kelly Jackson set him up.

"We adapted well to the artificial ice," Red Gadsby told reporters after the game. "And I don't believe we suffered from stage fright. I'm afraid we lacked a little leadership out there." Immediately Gadsby wanted to bite back the words, knowing they reflected badly on Max. But the truth was the truth.

Max declined all requests for interviews.

Red went to Max's room in the hotel. He found him lying on his bed, staring at the ceiling.

"What's the matter, kid? Something on your mind?" Red asked.

"I'll snap out of it, Red. I know I played a lousy game."

"Not much time left to snap out of it. We're down three goals with 60 minutes to play. You got a problem with that girl you've been seeing?"

"No, nothing like that."

But it wasn't the exact truth. The accusation of thievery, backed by evidence thrown at him in Mr. Gray's office, was certainly bad enough. But when he encountered Eileen on the street just before the train left for Boston, it was obvious she had learned what had happened.

"Max, how could you?" she had cried. "I can hardly believe it. And I won't be going to Boston."

There was less than a full house for the second game of the series. With total goals to count, the Cubs, with three goals to their credit, looked unbeatable. Who wants to pay good money to see a shellacking?

Max knew he'd done nothing in the first game. He knew he must find a way to overcome the terrible depression he'd felt from the moment he'd stumbled out of President Gray's office.

When the referee dropped the puck to start the second game, Max resolved to skate hard, to clear his mind, to regain his old form. This was his team's last chance and there was a huge lead to overcome.

But he was beaten on the first play when the opposing centreman won the draw, breezed past him and took a long shot at the Indian goal and almost scored. Less than ten seconds had elapsed.

"C'mon, Max!" shouted Marty. "Get with it!"

It was a speedy, rousing period and it was Kelly Jackson who made it so. Jackson hadn't fought all winter through one hard game after another to see his team get whitewashed in the final match.

Kelly made the expectations for the first line his own and for the first time in his life he was guilty of selfishness with the puck. His jaw set, he refused to send passes to Max. He preferred to battle his way down the boards and into the enemy zone on solo rushes and three times he almost scored.

Leclair, the Cub's top centreman, was having little trouble with Max. "Mitchell's a lot easier to handle than I expected," Leclair told his mates when he returned to the bench. "His passes to his wings are soft. We're intercepting most of them. And I've blocked two of his shots."

Five minutes before the period ended, Kelly Jackson found his reward. After Max had vainly tried to steal the puck away from Leclair, Kelly muscled his way in, grabbed the puck and cut loose with a brilliant rush straight down centre. At the Cub blue line he rifled a shot at Connor the Cub netminder. The rebound came off the goalie's chest and Jackson went after it, flinging two defenders aside as he swooped in. He scooped up the loose puck, deked

Connor and dumped the puck in behind him. Cubs 3; Indians 1.

Jackson's beautifully executed goal gave the Indians a lift. But it was not to last.

Right from the faceoff, Leclair outwitted Max with some clever stickhandling and shot wide of the Indians' net. A Cub winger roared in, beating Red Gadsby to the rebound. Leclair raced toward the net with Max on his heels. A hard pass skimmed across the ice and hit the tape of Leclair's stick. Max reached out, attempting to intercept. But he was a split second too late. Leclair calmly slid the puck into the open corner of the net behind Chubby and the Cubs had regained their three-goal lead.

"Shoulda had it," Max groaned. "I shoulda stopped that goal."

There was a heavy silence in the Indians' room when the players trooped in at the end of the period.

Max sat by himself in a corner, a towel over his head, his elbows on his knees. He was suffering through the most bitter moments of his life. He was letting his team down—and badly. He knew it and they knew it. Everyone knew it. For the life of him, he couldn't recapture that spark that had character-ized his play all season. His mental attitude was wrong—all wrong. But what could he do about it?

Red Gadsby came over and patted Max on the back. "You'll be all right, kid. We know you've got what it takes. There's still a little time left."

The others said nothing, but Max could sense their bitter disappointment. They couldn't understand how the one person they had always relied on for leadership was now failing them.

The silence was broken when Chubby Carlton wiped his face with a towel and snorted, "For Pete's sake, Max. What's eating you? If you're sick, tell us. If you're not, tell us why you're simply going through the motions..."

Just then the door flew open and a cheerful voice yelled, "Hi, ya, boys! What's going on? You holding a wake in here?"

It was Johnny Gray, as cheerful and as upbeat as ever. "I just got in and my cab driver got a ticket for breaking the speed limit getting me from the railway station to the rink. What's the score?"

"We're tied at one in this game, Johnny," someone said. "But we still trail by three in total goals."

"Don't worry, fellows. I know you'll catch fire. Say, Max, can I see you a moment out in the corridor."

Max got up and went into the corridor with his pal.

"Look here, Max," Johnny said quietly, "it's obvious there's something wrong with you. Where's the old Max Mitchell? What's the big problem?"

Max nodded miserably. "I know I'm playing rotten hockey, Johnny. I'm letting everybody down and I can't seem to do anything about it."

Johnny said earnestly, "Max, you got a raw deal back home. I came all the way here to tell you that. I didn't get the whole story out of my father until after the train left. He didn't want me to make the trip, see. But I know you didn't steal that money. It isn't in you to pull a stunt like that. Eileen agrees with me. She feels terrible she doubted you. There's been a frame-up somewhere. Sooner or later we'll find out who's behind it."

The referee passed them and banged on the dressing room door. He called out the three-minute warning.

Johnny grabbed Max by the arm. "My friend, you better get out there and fight. Think hockey—only hockey. And remember, Eileen and I are behind you all the way. Eileen knows how you covered up and wouldn't talk about the stranger in the restaurant because you didn't want to get her involved. That was noble. You're a great guy, Max. Believe it! You're the best thing that's happened to Indian River in years. Eileen sends her love, Max. And she means it. Now win this game—win it for her!"

Max felt as if a huge load had been lifted from his shoulders. Johnny Gray had come all this way just to tell him that he believed in his innocence. And Eileen believed in him too. He wondered how many others would believe it—that he could never be a thief.

CHAPTER 18

TIME FOR A COMEBACK

Three goals behind, two periods to play.

Max threw open the dressing room door and strode to the bench. He grabbed his stick and his gloves. He startled his mates with his shout. "Let's go, men! Let's beat the tar out of the Cubs!"

Chubby Carlton whacked his goal stick against the floor. "That's more like it, pal. That's what we need to hear from you. Now show us that you mean it."

High in the broadcasting booth above the ice surface, a bored radio play-by-play announcer summed up the first period: "The Cubs appear to be a cinch to move on to the finals against the Supremes, folks. They shutout the Indians three to nothing in the first game of this series and they still hold a three-goal margin with 40 minutes to play. The lads from Indian River are trying hard but they're outclassed. And their star centreman, Max Mitchell, has gone stale. Perhaps the dual role of player and coach has been too much of a burden for him."

The announcer would soon note that it was a different Max Mitchell who skated out to centre ice for the second period. He had thrown off his lethargy. Thanks to Johnny's appeal and Chubby's outburst, he'd regained his senses—and his focus. "Think hockey—and only hockey," Johnny had told him. It was great advice. And he owed something to the team that had been so loyal to him all season, a team that he'd surely been letting down.

Leclair, the opposing centreman, had won every draw from Max and fully expected to lead off the period by doing so again. But Max tied up Leclair and gained control of the puck, which he passed off to Jackson. Max took a return pass and shifted right through the two defenceman, who were caught napping.

The fans were still settling in their seats when Max rifled a shot at Connor, which sent the goalie staggering. Max raced in before Connor could begin to think of clearing the rebound. He snapped a wicked shot right through the bewildered goalie's legs. The red light flashed at the same instant Max piled into the end boards with a crash that could be heard all through the arena and out in the parking lot. For a split second, there was silence. Then a great roar went up from the Indian River fans.

From that moment, the complexion of the game

changed. The goal was a turning point. Max was back—the old Max—playing as he had never played before.

Leclair found himself tied up in knots. His wingers ran into aggressive checkers every time they touched the puck, which was less and less often. "What's gotten into that guy?" Leclair asked when he reached his team's bench, winded and bewildered.

The Indians were no longer playing a defensive game. Max led a series of brilliant rushes that left the Cubs gasping. They were swept off their feet, rattled and disorganized by this terrific, sustained rally.

A Cub winger, frustrated at his inability to hold Kelly Jackson in check, lost his head and yanked Kelly's feet out from under him.

"Two minutes!" bellowed the ref.

The Cub coach sent out his top defenders and Max countered by placing Sammy Fox and Barry Miller at the points. Miller had proven himself an outstanding team player and displayed a wonderful new attitude. Max could now rely on him in any situation.

Eager for another goal, the Indians swarmed in. It came in a minute and a half, with at least four players sprawled on the ice and the Cub goalie floundering in his net. Max plucked the puck from among the fallen bodies, heard Miller holler, "Max! Max!" and put the disc on Miller's stick as he drove in from the blue line. Miller's sizzling shot hit the twine and there was bedlam in the arena.

The Cubs lead had been reduced to a single goal on the round and the Cubs morale had been reduced to ashes.

At full strength, the Cubs tried to battle back. But their attack crumbled at the Indian blue line where Red Gadsby and Jim McEvoy were waiting. Red joyously sent an incoming forward into the boards, then, with a whoop, hoisted him right over the boards and into the lap of a heavyset matron who wore Indian River colours. She threw her arms around the interloper and refused to let him go. The harder he struggled, the tighter her grip and finally, the referee stopped play. The Cub forward hustled back over the boards, indignant and embarrassed.

A voice cried out, "Marry him, Myrtle!" Everybody laughed and Myrtle stood and bowed in all directions.

Moments later, the same forward, looking for vengeance, charged at Red, but the canny defence-man threw out a hip and sent him flying through the air. The Cub was once again the butt of many laughs and headed straight for the bench.

Red saw Max break away with the puck and raced up ice to join him. His gamble paid off when Max sidestepped one check, faked a shot and sent a perfect pass skimming across the ice to the redhead.

Gadsby took it and fired blindly, all in one motion. Connor got his glove up, but the puck might have been fired from a cannon. The shot knocked Connor's glove off and both glove and puck wound up deep inside the goal net.

Three goals in less than 15 minutes! The Indians had tied a series that most fans had decided was hopelessly lost. In the broadcast booth, the play-by-play announcer was on his feet, his voice now almost hoarse. "They scored! They scored! This is unbelievable, folks. The crowd has gone wild. The Cubs have fallen apart. This kid Mitchell has led the Indians on an incredible comeback. And it's not over yet."

Back in Indian River, where a thousand ears were bent to the radio broadcast, incredulous delight prevailed.

Resting briefly on the Indian bench, Max barked at Kelly and Peewee, "Come on, guys! Come on! We've got the jump on them. We've got to get the go-ahead goal in this period. If we let them go to the dressing room with the round still tied, they'll have a chance to regroup. And they're still mighty dangerous."

The game went into high gear again when Max and his linemates skated out. Max shook himself free of a desperate Leclair and banged a long, low shot against the rear boards behind Connor. He had figured out those boards by now and knew the angle of rebound. Kelly Jackson flew into the enemy zone the moment Max took his shot. He swept around the Cub defence and snapped up the disc as it skimmed out from the boards. The angle was tight but just enough to permit a shot and Kelly didn't hesitate. While falling to his knees, he drilled one at Connor who miraculously kicked it aside. Peewee Halloran charged in for the rebound, snared it and shot wildly at the net. The puck struck the knob of Conner's goal stick and fell into the crease. Max came racing in from the sideboards and golfed the puck high into the corner of the cage.

From all the radios in Indian River came the hysterical announcement: "He scores! Mitchell has scored for Indian River! For the first time, the Indians have taken the lead. Don't turn that dial. Don't go to bed yet, folks. We're bringing you one of the greatest games ever played, certainly one of the most exciting periods of hockey this old boy has ever seen. And there are 20 minutes still to come. There's the bell ending the second period. Time for me to take a breather."

In the dressing room, Johnny Gray gave Max a slap on the back that knocked him against the wall. "Am I glad to be here to see this," he exclaimed. "I thought I was going to have 14 heart attacks watching you fellas perform."

Red Gadsby nudged Max in the ribs. "What got into you out there? You were ten times the player you were in the opener."

Max grinned back at him. "We can't disappoint Johnny," he said.

Red chuckled. "Yeah, and Johnny's sister. If she was here, we might be 20 goals ahead."

"Be quiet," Max said, blushing. "Put a sock in it."

The second period scoring binge took the heart out of the Cubs. They skated hard in the final frame, but their passing and shooting was ineffective. Max and Kelly Jackson broke away at the seven-minute mark, and while Kelly pulled the Cub defenceman out of position, Max accelerated and broke for the net. Kelly whistled a pass over to him, and Max deflected the puck over Connor's outstretched leg. It was a beautiful goal and Max made it look easy.

"There's your hat trick!" Kelly shouted as he threw his arms around his centreman.

In the final minute, the Cubs called their goalie to the bench. It was a new strategy to hockey—leaving the net empty and sending out an extra attacker—and many arguments had developed over the wisdom of the strategy. The Cub coach shrugged as if to say, "What can we lose?"

For most of the minute, a battle raged in front of Chubby Carlton. Players flew at each other. They grunted and groaned and sticks clashed. With ten seconds to play, the puck squirted loose and Max scooped it up. Calmly, he hoisted it high in the air, a backhand shot. For a moment it looked like it might hit the clock over centre ice. Then it dropped slowly to the ice, bounced twice and slid slowly over the goal line into the empty net. The goal came at 19:58.

The Cubs had had enough. They dashed to their dressing room, throwing their sticks in frustration at the corridor walls and refusing to play the final two seconds. They ignored the traditional post-game handshakes.

The crowd, cheated by two seconds of seeing a complete game, had been thoroughly entertained and rose to give the winners a spontaneous roar of approval. The Indians, in stunning fashion, had advanced to the Cup finals when nobody had given them a worm's chance in a fishpond of ever getting there.

CHAPTER 19

HARD HIT BY INJURIES

The Indians didn't come out of the struggle with the Cubs unscathed. The hockey highway leading to the junior title is always strewn with casualties and the Indians were going to have to carry on with some players on the limp. Marshall, left-winger on the second line, was nursing a cracked rib. Jim McEvoy had a badly bruised shoulder. Kelly Jackson was nursing a split lip and a black eye. Max himself was black and blue from the roughhouse tactics of the Cubs.

None of the Indians complained. They were all young and in good shape and able to shake off the effects of their injuries quickly. And they were comforted by the knowledge that their final opponents of the season, the Ridgeway Supremes, had also travelled a rocky road on their way to the top.

The Indians' surprise victory over the highly rated Cubs had gained them some hockey fame. In the two-day interval before their first engagement with the Supremes, the newspaper accounts of their success were glowing. Max came in for more attention than he thought he deserved. While he didn't mind talking about his play against the Cubs, he was more concerned with how he and his mates would do when they encountered the Supremes. They were a team packed with "imports," the best young hockey stars available, brought into Ridgeway at great expense. They had lost only two games all season, both on a weekend when Charlie Bower, their all-star goaltender, had to attend a funeral. The coach, Cap Blake, had piloted three Stanley Cup winners in his time.

On the sports page, Pete Clarke asked the question:

Can the kids from Indian River do it? Do they have any chance at all?

Doesn't seem so. It's amateurs versus shamateurs. You see, every player on the Supremes is slated for a professional tryout next fall. Two of them—Apps and Cowley—may finish one-two as NHL rookie of the year.

Give the Indians credit. They polished off the Cubs after nobody gave them a snowball's chance. But can they repeat against this well-drilled, experienced, fast, hard-hitting aggregation? Not likely. But anything can happen in hockey.

The arena was sold out for the best-of-three series. A large crowd of Indian River fans had rushed to the city by train to battle for tickets to the big event.

Max watched the Supremes during a workout on the eve of the game. "We'll have our hands full," he told Johnny Gray. "No weaknesses that I can see on that club. And they're all huge men, especially Apps and Cowley."

"The bigger they are, the harder they fall, is what I always say," Johnny answered with a laugh. "They're no bigger than some of the seniors you played against this season."

The crowd began to whoop it up ten minutes before the opening faceoff for game one. By the time the puck was dropped the noise level had reached such a peak that fans were holding their ears.

The pace in the opening period was as fast as in any pro game. These kids could skate! Max and his mates were in every way equal to the Supremes starting line, perhaps even faster, but the Supremes had been taught to soften up opponents with solid body-checking. The Indian River subs took quite a hammering. So did Gadsby and McEvoy, who appeared to be on the receiving end of every vicious body-slam, sneaky elbow and slash to the legs.

The first break came in the third period—and the Supremes got it. Apps, a marvelous skater, stick-handled his way in and scooted around Gadsby, who stumbled and fell. Apps had a clear opening to the net and rifled a shot past Chubby for the opening goal.

Two minutes later—another break went to the Supremes. Two players formed a screen in front of Chubby and Cowley's long shot from the blue line hopped crazily along the ice. It struck a rut, changed direction and fell into the net. Chubby never saw it until the red light flashed.

The Indians didn't give up. But they couldn't score a goal. Bower played a strong game and robbed them several times. Time ran out in the third period with a wild scramble around Bower's crease. Just before the buzzer, Max drilled a rising shot off the crossbar, the puck deflecting high into the crowd.

At the end of the game, someone overheard Coach Blake say, "I told you they'd fall apart if we hit them hard. You'll see more of the same next game."

On the afternoon of the second game, Red Gadsby called Max on the phone. "Come on down to 318 right away," he ordered. "We've got a problem."

Max hurried down the stairs and entered the room. There was Kelly Jackson, still in bed, a cold compress on his forehead. Gadsby was at his side. "Kelly's really sick. It may be his appendix."

"Let's get him over to the hospital," Max said. "Call a taxi!"

At the hospital, doctors took a long time examining their patient. Finally, one of them told Max and

Red they were going to keep Kelly over night, and maybe for a day or two after that.

"Call the hospital tomorrow," the medical men said.

The hotel lobby was thronged with Indian River fans who had arrived on the afternoon train. Max looked for Eileen in the crowd but didn't see her. He did see Myron Seymour who ran over and shook Max by the hand.

"We're all pulling for you, Max."

"Sure you are," Max murmured as he turned away. "Pulling for us but putting all your money on the Supremes. I know your act, Seymour."

It was inevitable that Jackson's absence would be noted. When the players learned about his illness, they were crushed. He was a valuable man and they regarded his absence from the lineup as a deathblow to their chances of tying the series.

The rink that night was a colourful sight as the teams skated out for their warm-up. Tier upon tier of seats was jammed to capacity. A huge block of Indian River fans, wearing the team colours, made a noisy racket with cowbells, horns and whistles. A trumpeter among them threatened to puncture eardrums with periodic blasts on his instrument.

Max had a talk with Peewee just before they went out on the ice. "We'll have to move Barry Miller or Sammy Fox up to the first line to replace Kelly. But that'll weaken the rest of the club. And neither

Sammy nor Barry is in Kelly's class. Nobody is..."

"Wait a minute," Max said, rising to his feet. He walked over to where Johnny Gray was sitting next to Chubby.

He grabbed Johnny by the tie and led him from the room. In the corridor he pinned him to the wall.

"Listen, Johnny, all season I've let you skate with the boys. You're a terrific player and we all know it. You say your dad won't allow you to play hockey. Well, your dad has done everything he can to destroy hockey in our town. He's even accused me of stealing from him. You're a man now. Are you going to let your dad dictate how you live your life? I suggest you start making some decisions on your own. We need you and we need you now. Kelly Jackson's uniform is in his stall and I suggest you get into it. Tell your old man he's crazy if he thinks he can make you jump through hoops for the rest of your life."

Johnny could only gape at Max.

"I'm bolting the dressing room door in 30 seconds, Johnny. That's how much time you have to make up your mind."

Max sat quietly on the bench in the dressing room. Fifteen seconds passed, then 20. He started toward the door when it burst open. Johnny flew in, all out of breath. "I had to grab my skates in the lobby. Left them there behind the ticket counter—just in case..."

"Hot dog!" he cried, "I'm now an Indian!"

The Indians gave him a royal welcome.

The noise from the stands was deafening when the teams skated out. Max faced off against Latimer, a top pro prospect, known far and wide for his mean streak. "Keep your head up, busher!" he told Max as they moved in for the faceoff. "Don't worry about me, hot shot!" Max replied.

The drop of the puck, the clash of sticks, the great roar of the crowd and the game was underway.

On the very first play, Max got the puck across to Johnny Gray, who spun away from his check and streaked up the ice only to run into a thunderous bodycheck.

"I'll remember that," he said, pointing a finger at his opponent. "Got your number. I'll be back." The player thumbed his nose at Johnny.

"Mad Dog" Michaels, a 200-pound rushing defenceman, led a return rush for the Supremes and crashed deliberately into Peewee Halloran, slamming the jockey-sized player into the boards. Halloran was out cold and had to be carried to the dressing room. It was a brutal, unsportsmanlike piece of work and it left Max cold with fury. Michaels laughed as he went to the penalty box.

"Five minutes," hollered the ref. "Deliberate intent to injure." Michaels sneered at the referee and held his arms out to the crowd, a gesture of innocence. "Why me?" he asked them. "I didn't touch the guy."

So that was how the Supremes played hockey, Max thought. Not content with moulding a packed team of salaried players, not content with ignoring all the principles of amateurism, they also resorted to bullying tactics and laughed in the faces of those they trampled and tormented.

Max called on Sammy Fox to replace Halloran.

Max looked into the eyes of Latimer as they crouched for the faceoff.

"So that's how you city slickers win your games," Max sneered. "Try to kill the little guys. That penalty to Michaels is going to cost you guys."

"That so, busher? Well, let's see what you've got. It can't be much."

Max trapped the puck when it fell, shoved it between Latimer's legs, darted around him and picked it up, then raced toward the blue line.

A Supreme defenceman leaped at him, intent on crushing him to the ice. Max sidestepped neatly as the man sprawled foolishly into a teammate, knocking him bow-legged. Max powered in, saw Bower, the all-star goalie, crouching, waiting. "Stop this, Bower!" he yelled as he unleashed a vicious shot that smoked its way into the back of the net. Bower hadn't moved a muscle. The goalie had seemed paralyzed by the bullet-like drive.

The red light blinked. The roar that went up from ten thousand throats seemed to lift the roof off the building.

Max skated back, mobbed by his backslapping mates. One short-handed goal. It was a start.

"I'm next," Johnny Gray said to Max before the faceoff. "Get me the puck, then sit back and watch."

Johnny had starred on his prep-school team and still held school records for scoring. The Supremes had no idea his talent matched or surpassed anyone else's on the ice. They paid scant attention to the newcomer.

Latimer won the draw and tossed the puck deep into the Indians' zone. Johnny Gray raced back for it and circled the net. Then he started a solo rush that would be talked about for weeks after the season. He dodged a checker who tried to slash his legs out from under him, dashed up the sideboards and stickhandled brilliantly around Latimer, who tried to grab him by the jersey and couldn't hang on.

He pushed the puck through the legs of the right winger and moved in on the defence. He faked going inside, pulled away and went outside, streaking past both defenders as they tried to haul him down. Bower jumped into action, threw out a long poke check. Too late. Johnny Gray laughed as he whipped a shot over Bower's head, the puck almost parting his hair, as it found the back of the net.

Indians 2, Supremes 0.

Johnny's goal gave the Indians some much-needed confidence. Johnny Gray not only scored two more goals but he took time to settle a score of another kind. In the third period, the defenceman who had rattled him with a check on the very first shift circled his net and skated full speed up the ice. He looked down at the puck for an instant and that's when Johnny Gray cut into his path and delivered a check that shook the building. Johnny's victim flew in the air, gloves and stick sailing in all directions. He somersaulted back to the ice where he lay moaning and groaning, barely conscious.

"Sorry, bud," Johnny said, leaning over him. "But I warned you, didn't I?"

With the lead, the Indians checked tenaciously and totally frustrated Apps and Cowley, who were marked men from start to finish.

Johnny Gray, fresh and eager, was the star of the game. He added extra punch to Max's line and his three goals may have been the difference between defeat and victory. Final score: Indians 5, Supremes 2.

After fighting their way through a mob of cheering supporters, the Indians rested in their dressing room. They exchanged short phrases: "Great game, Chubby!"; "Nice work, Max"; "You were terrific, Johnny. That peabrain you hit may not wake up until Tuesday, ha ha."

Max sipped a cold drink and thought about the future. With the series tied, one more game stood between the Indians and the junior championship. In a few short weeks, he and his mates had come a long way down the hockey highway. They were almost at the end of it now. There was one more obstacle in their path.

CHAPTER 20

ANOTHER COMPLICATION

On the following morning, Johnny Gray met Max in the hotel coffee shop. He carried a newspaper in his hand and his face was flushed with anger. "Look at this, fellas," he said, tossing the sports page on the table. Max and Marty read the item:

Johnny Gray, a surprise starter for the Indians and the individual star in last night's dramatic win over the Supremes, may have some explaining to do when he gets back home. His father, President Gray of the Indian River paper mill, denied his son permission to play for the Indians earlier this season. Mr. Gray has consistently refused to support the team. What's more, it is rumoured that he has banned playing-coach Max Mitchell from company property after a sum of money that disappeared from the company coffers wound up in the treasury of the hockey club. He refrained from accusing Mitchell of stealing the money but he did say, "Mr. Mitchell was on the premises when it went missing."

Gray ordered his son Johnny to decline any invitations to join the Indians, an edict his son ignored when he played in last night's game. More fireworks are bound to follow.

Max whistled. "So they're coming out and branding me a thief."

"Somebody gave that item to the paper," Johnny declared. "You and I know that only a handful of people in Indian River knew about those 50-dollar bills. Somebody in town is trying to stir up a lot of trouble..."

"Myron Seymour?" asked Max.

"That's what I thought at first. But I can't see it. They tell me he won a pot of money on last night's game betting on the Indians."

"And I thought he was wagering against us," Max answered. Max stared at the newspaper thoughtfully. "So the secret is out at last," he sighed. "Now everybody will assume I stole that money."

"Listen," Johnny said. "Try not to worry about it. Maybe the Supremes are behind this nonsense, trying to get to you. Remember, just think hockey." The advice was sound, but difficult to follow. Max became conscious of people in the lobby whispering amongst themselves when he walked by. When a couple of reporters approached him he said, "No comment, fellas," and hurried through the revolving doors.

On the street, a drunken Supremes fan recognized him and cackled, "Stop, thief!" from across the street, as if it was a big joke. Max walked around the block to cool off, then returned to his room. He lay down but he couldn't sleep. Win or lose, he would play one more game for Indian River.

The phone rang.

"Is this Max Mitchell?"

"Yes, it is."

"Could I see you downstairs for a minute. It's important."

"Who is this?"

"I'm the fella who gave you the donation for your team—up in Hartley. Remember? Maybe you'd like to talk to me."

"I'll be right down," Max said, slamming down the receiver.

The heavyset man in the blue coat and brown hat was standing beside the newspaper stand when Max reached the lobby. "Let's go somewhere quiet where we can talk," the stranger said, starting toward the lobby doors. "I saw that stuff in the paper about you being crooked. I can help."

Max followed at his heels. "You're the one man on earth who can clear my name," he said. "That donation of yours put me in a terrible situation."

Max glanced around and saw Johnny Gray sitting in one of the lobby chairs. Johnny frowned and called out to Max. "Where you headed, pal? I thought you were taking a nap."

"Got some business to attend to, Johnny. I'll be back soon."

The stranger led Max down the street and around a corner. He stopped in front of a poolroom. "Let's go in here," he said. "I'll explain everything."

Max was bursting with questions. Who was this guy? Where did he get those 50-dollar bills he'd given Max?

The man led Max between several pool tables, down a hallway and into a small room. Max was surprised to see two heavy men sitting at a table, smoking cigars and drinking beer. "Come in, come in," the stranger urged, when he saw Max hanging back. He pulled Max into the room and closed the door behind him.

The man moved close to Max, so close Max could smell the liquor on his breath. "My name's Dewar," he said. Suddenly, his voice was a lot less friendly. "These men are pals of mine."

"Hi," Max said. The two men at the table grunted in response. One of them grinned and blew a thick smoke ring in his direction.

Dewar pointed a finger at Max. "Now listen to me, fella. Me and my friends stand to lose a bundle of money if your team wins the big game tonight."

"What are you getting at?" Max asked nervously.

He wondered if he should turn and bolt for the door, but the man named Dewar was half-blocking his way.

"Listen, Mitchell," he snarled. "I lost big money on your game in Hartley because someone in your own camp told me the outcome was a sure thing—that you'd lose big. Why? Because he switched the station tag on your equipment box, forcing you and your players to use borrowed gear that night. Second-rate equipment. But he made a big mistake. He didn't send your equipment box far enough up the line and you got it back in time to win the game."

Max was beginning to put things together. "That would be Seymour, right?"

"Yeah, that's the name. Like me, Seymour lost a bundle that night betting against the Indians. And see, it wasn't his own dough—it was company money he used. He was in a big jam and he came to me. He said we could use some money he stole from the company cash box to frame you, to set you up. He said it would put your team out of the running and ruin your reputation. That's why I gave you those four fifties I got from Seymour."

Max felt an icy feeling in the pit of his stomach. "So Seymour was the thief."

"Yeah. The guy's addicted to gambling and he's been dipping into company funds on and off for a long time."

"So why are you telling me this?" Max asked, fearful of the answer.

"You want your name cleared, right?"

"Of course. That would be nice."

"All right. Consider it done. Just don't show up at the rink tonight."

Max stared at him. He almost laughed. "You're kidding. You know I've got to show up at the rink."

Once again Dewar wagged a thick finger at Max. "Don't you get it, bud? This guy Seymour has cost me plenty. He guaranteed me your club would lose to the Supremes last night. He even tipped off the Supremes' coach to send his players after Halloran and put him out of the game. Halloran's small and you're always setting him up for goals. But you and that Gray kid screwed everything up. The only consolation I got was that Seymour lost a pot full of money, too."

"But I heard he won money—betting on us to win."

"Not true," snorted Dewar. "He bragged about winning a big bet on you fellas, but that was to show people he was behind you all the way. He really lost a bundle betting on the Supremes. Now he's counting on a sure thing—and so are we—and that means the Indians have to lose tonight."

Max glanced back at the door. He wondered if Dewar had somehow locked it. He told himself to stay cool, to look for a way out of this situation.

Then he said to Dewar, "So if I don't show up for the game tonight and the Supremes win, you'll make a killing. So will your friends here and so will Seymour…"

Dewar laughed. "Yeah, but I'm going to take care of that bum Seymour. It'll be a nice surprise. I plan to go to old man Gray and tell him the truth about Seymour. You'll be cleared and Seymour will be toast. He has it coming to him, don't you think?"

The other men in the room stared at Max through a cloud of cigar smoke. They smiled when they heard Dewar's plan. Max thought they both looked like rats. Vicious, cigar-chomping rats.

Max stalled for time. He knew he was in a trap. He could clear his name, but only at the expense of his team. Did Dewar think he'd actually agree to such a thing? Miss the big game? Make a deal with a double-crossing thug like Dewar and his cronies? Stoop to their level? It was unthinkable.

"If I don't show up, my teammates will think I ran out on them," he suggested.

"We can provide a good reason for you not playing," Dewar said, a sly grin crossing his fat face.

"Like?"

"Like a little accident. You could suffer a broken wrist just leaving this place. Couldn't he, boys?" The two thugs grinned and nodded. One of them pushed his chair back and stood up.

Looks like a wrestler, Max thought. And the other one isn't much smaller. And they're both as ugly as alligators. Max calculated the distance to the door. If he moved fast, he could reach the knob. But was the door locked? He shouted, "Nothing doing, you slimeballs." Then he spun around and yanked the door partially open. He was quick and he almost made it. But Dewar, for a big man, was fast, too. He flung himself at Max and brought him down with a tackle. Max struggled fiercely, but the other two men pounced on him too. One of them slammed the door shut with his foot. They dragged Max across the room and threw him in a chair.

Dewar's face was as red as a radish. "Okay, pal. You just made a huge mistake. You won't be playin' hockey tonight and maybe never again. We're going to break every bone in your body, punk. Go to work on him, boys."

The thugs moved in, but Max got a leg free and lashed out with it, catching one of his assailants in the groin. The man fell back, knocked his companion off balance and crashed into the table. Coffee flew out of the cups. Max swung an elbow and caught the second man in the jaw, breaking a couple of teeth. The man howled and cursed and swung his big fist at Max's head. Max ducked and took the blow on his shoulder. He threw a hard right hand into the man's face and blood spurted out of his nose. Dewar joined the fight and leaped on Max's back. The other two pummelled him in the face and stomach. Max went down under the weight of Dewar. The man with the bleeding nose grabbed Max by the wrist. He tried to force it back, tried to break it. Max lashed out with his left hand and punched him in the nose for the second time. More blood flowed and, howling, the man released his hold on Max's wrist.

Suddenly, above the uproar, there was a commotion at the door. It crashed open and through a crimson mist, Max saw Red Gadsby leading a charge of furious hockey players into the room. Red grabbed one of the thugs by the throat and tossed him into a wall, cracking the plaster. Johnny Gray leaped across the room at Dewar and smacked him on the side of the head with a big fist. The room was full of players, all trying to get their licks in and rescue their leader. Chubby Carlton and Sammy Fox helped Max to his feet. Marty was there, too.

"You all right, Max?" Marty asked, pulling a handkerchief from a pocket and wiping blood from his brother's face. At the same time, he turned to kick Dewar squarely in the behind with his foot.

"I'm pretty sore," Max admitted, feeling the bruises on his face and flexing his wrist. "But I don't think anything's broken."

The thugs lay on the floor, cowering. Marty broke

the tension by snarling at them. "If you guys move a muscle, I'll beat the stuffing out of you."

Marty's threat caused Max to smile through swollen lips. In the distance, police sirens screamed.

CHAPTER 21

THE END OF THE HIGHWAY

When the Indians skated out to face the Supremes for the junior championship that night, the fans, jammed into every corner of the big arena, rocked the building with a huge roar of support.

The moment Max stepped on the ice, nursing a black eye and a bloody nose, a block of Supremes rooters set up a chant: "Thief! Thief! Thief!" and "Where's the money, Mitchell? Where's the money?"

A fan rushed up to harass Max from rinkside. He leaned over, waving a handful of bills at Max and shouted, "Want some more money, kid? Want some more?"

The next time Max circled the ice he "accidentally" shot out the blade of his stick and knocked the bills from the man's hand. They went flying into the stands and people scrambled after them. "Hey, that's my dough," the man cried, dropping to his knees to get back what he could. The crowd howled with laughter.

The Supremes were tense and jittery when the game began. They knew their fancy reputation was at stake and a national title depended on their performance over the next 60 minutes. For the first time all season, they showed real respect for—and some real fear of—their small town opponents.

As for Max and the Indians, they showed no indication of nervousness. They'd been in a real-life battle earlier in the day and emerged triumphant. Their adrenalin was flowing again as they began the final step toward the title.

For the first time in many days, Max felt as free as a bird. And much of the credit went to Johnny Gray. That afternoon, Johnny had become suspicious of the man who'd escorted Max out of the hotel. The stranger matched the description of a man his sister had told him about, the fellow who'd conversed with Max after the game in Hartley. It was the brown hat that Johnny remembered.

Johnny left the hotel lobby and trailed Max and the stranger to the poolroom. Suspecting something fishy, he returned to the hotel and rounded up his teammates. They raced back, invaded the premises and rescued Max from a beating that would surely have put him in the hospital had it continued any longer.

Unfortunately, one of the players had been

injured in the ruckus. Chubby Carlton had twisted an ankle and was limping so badly he would not be able to play in the final game. "Then my brother Marty will play in goal," Max said. "We'll miss Chubby, but don't worry about Marty hurting us. He'll be fine."

There was no holding the Indians in the first period. They crashed through their opponents and their superior speed carried them through to Bower's goal crease. Only his superb goaltending kept the Indians off the scoresheet. But he couldn't deny the Indians forever. Before the game was ten minutes old, Max took a long lead pass from Johnny Gray and left a Supremes defenceman spinning with a deceptive move. He dashed in and drilled a shot to the corner. Short side goal! Charlie Bower went sprawling. The Indians took the lead.

In the dying moments of the period, Max set up Johnny. His short pass hit the tape on Johnny's stick and a quick flick of Johnny's wrists directed the puck into the net. "Attaboy, Johnny," Max shrieked in his linemate's ear as they embraced. Charlie Bower looked on in disgust, then turned and slammed his goal stick across the crossbar, shattering it into 100 pieces.

Over the roar of the crowd, fans back in Indian River strained to hear the announcement on their radios. In the Mitchell residence, Harry Mitchell said,

"I'd give anything to be there tonight. If I didn't have a newspaper to publish tomorrow..."

His wife said, "I can't believe little Marty is playing goal against those big bruisers. I'm so afraid he'll get hurt."

"Folks," the announcer went on, "the lads from Indian River are proving their great performance in game two was no fluke. They look even stronger tonight, especially Mitchell and Gray. The Indians have played short-handed twice and Sammy Fox just put on a brilliant display of stickhandling to kill time. And believe me, this kid in goal, Marty Mitchell, the youngest player on the ice, has been unbeatable. What a surprise he's been! And so, at the end of 20 minutes, it's two to nothing Indians."

When the players trooped off to their dressing rooms, Max caught sight of a familiar face near the gate waving her program frantically. "Max! Max!"

"Why didn't you tell me Eileen was coming to the game?" Max asked Johnny, poking him with an elbow.

"I didn't know," Johnny protested. "Honest. Good gosh, there's Dad with her."

Outside the dressing room, Eileen gave both Max and her brother a kiss for good luck and Mr. Gray extended his hand to Max. "I owe you an apology, young man," he said. "I'll talk to you more about it later but I want you to know how sorry I am that I misjudged you. Perhaps I misjudged many things."

"That's all right, sir," said Max. "But how did you know?"

"I have my contacts and I know the full story about Seymour and the missing money."

"I convinced Dad he should come down on the afternoon train with me," Eileen said. "And I never want to see Myron again for as long as I live. But Max, what in the world happened to your face? I didn't see you get hit."

"I'll tell you all about it after the game," Max said. "And how your brother here saved my butt."

Johnny glanced sheepishly at his father. "You still mad at me, Dad? I couldn't resist joining the team. I've never been happier."

"Mad at you? I'm proud of you. You're one of the best players out there. Imagine! My only son—a hockey star!"

Johnny threw an arm around his father's shoulder. "Thanks, Dad. Now watch my dust in the second period."

"Oh, man, I'll never be able to keep up with him now," Max said, winking at Eileen.

Johnny Gray was unstoppable in the second period. And Max, with Eileen cheering his every move, was just as spectacular. Between them, they scored four goals. Between them, they put the game out of reach.

Fans agreed the Supremes had too much firepower to be shut out. They had averaged four or more goals per game all season. And they had some glorious chances against the Indians. But a bundle of energy in goal stopped shot after shot, many of which appeared to be certain lamplighters.

At the end of the period, the crowd gave Marty Mitchell a standing ovation and Max skated over to give him a brotherly hug. "You're stealing the spotlight, Marty," he kidded. "Save a little for the rest of us."

"I told you I was better than Ardath," Marty replied. "I'm glad the silly bugger quit."

"Hey, watch your language," Max said, making a painful stab at grinning. His jaw was still plenty sore. "And don't let a little success go to your head. I'll say this: So far, you're the best player on the ice."

"Well, I expect to be, every time I play," was Marty's response. "I love beating forwards who think I'm half-blind or as awkward as a kid on stilts. You're not the only hockey player in the family, you know."

Max slapped his brother on the shoulder. "I know it now. I've never been more proud of you, pal. And I expect a lot more of the same in the final period."

Marty turned in another superb performance in the final 20 minutes, while Max and his mates checked the Supremes to a standstill. Their aim now was to preserve Marty's shutout.

The Supremes didn't quit. But they were deflated

and discouraged. They knew their season would end on a dismal note. The score was six to nothing when the buzzer signalled the end of play. The Indians threw their sticks and gloves aside and piled on Marty. They embraced each other and suddenly they found themselves embracing a man in street clothes who'd raced out to congratulate them. It was Steve Kennedy, the coach who'd started them along the hockey highway. Steve joined the line as the Supremes, who were all good sports, lined up to shake hands with the winners.

Apps, Cowley and Bower gathered around Max. "You're some hockey player," Bower said. "I never knew what you were going to do next in front of my goal."

"Charlie's right, kid," said Apps. "We might have won if you hadn't been playing against us—you and that Gray character. He's almost in your class."

"Don't forget the kid brother in goal," Bower added. "He was sensational."

Cowley pumped Max by the hand once more. "You've got a great future ahead of you, Mitchell," he said, smiling through a cut lip. "You play hard and you play fair. I like that. I hope we meet again."

"It's a wonderful tradition, isn't it?" Steve Kennedy said to Max as they joined the Indians for more hugging and backslapping. "Winners and losers shaking hands after a title game. It's a hockey tradition. You don't see it in other team sports."

The fans remained standing, cheering and clapping. Over the din, Steve told Max, "I'm so proud of you, my boy. You did a marvellous job with this team."

"You showed me the way, coach," Max replied.

It was the end of a long season and the beginning of a lengthy celebration for the Indians who scampered around the ice hugging friends, strangers and each other, for the ice was now jammed with people who wanted to share in the excitement. When the Indians were grouped together for a team photo, the crowd rose as one and let loose a tumultuous roar of acclaim for the new champions.

Afterward, the Indians' dressing room was packed with fans from the paper town, mill workers beaming with pride for their boys. Only then did Max learn that his team had narrowly escaped a committee room decision that might have cost them that hard-won second game—and the title.

Mr. Gray explained what happened. "When you used Johnny on wing in the second game, the Supremes wanted to lodge a protest. Their claim was that Johnny was ineligible. His name wasn't on the official scoresheet prior to the game."

"And they'd have been right," Max said. "They'd have won their protest. But why didn't they?"

"Well," Mr. Gray went on, "I got on the phone and called the manager of the Supremes. I told him if he went ahead with his protest I'd hire detectives to investigate all the players on the Supremes. I told him they weren't amateurs, they were men being paid well to play the game. I told him I'd probably find enough dirt to have his club tossed out of hockey."

"So you were rooting for us all the time!" Johnny declared.

Mr. Gray smiled. "If I hadn't been so bullheaded, I'd have been rooting for you a lot earlier. I didn't help much. You boys won on your own merits. You whipped a couple of the best teams around. And if I ever lay my hands on that scoundrel Seymour…" But he never did. Seymour had disappeared faster than a magician's coin, leaving several exasperated gamblers threatening to tear him limb from limb if they ever crossed paths with him again.

Max managed to slip away from the backslapping crowd in the dressing room. In the corridor, he found Eileen waiting for him, her eyes glowing with happiness. "Max, I'm so glad you discovered my father's not such an ogre after all. Never again will you have trouble getting him to support your hockey team—or your dreams."

"It seems I'm never short of dreams, am I?"

"No, and from the look on your face I'll bet you've already got another one in mind."

"I do, Eileen. In the Boston area alone there are a

number of outstanding college teams. Even though your father offered me a good job in the mill after high school, I think I'd like to talk to some college coaches. I think I'd be a pretty good student athlete. I've never taken money to play the game so I'd be eligible. I know my folks would be thrilled if I carried on with my education."

"And so would I," Eileen replied, taking him by the arm and leading him down the corridor. "Even if it takes you to a college far away." She smiled at him, moisture in her eyes.

"Hey, the season's over," Max howled in happiness, his voice echoing off the walls. "Time to celebrate. Let's go buy the biggest ice cream sundaes we can find."

"I heard that," a voice behind them called out. "Wait for me." They turned to see Marty running to catch up.

"Make mine a banana split," he said, grinning broadly. "With…"

"I know, I know," Max said, throwing one arm around his brother's shoulder. "With three kinds of ice cream, loads of whipped cream and three red cherries on top. My treat, little brother. You've earned it."

Eileen laughed and took each brother by the hand, squeezing hard. "Let's go, my hockey heroes."

LOOKING AHEAD

When the Mitchell brothers are invited to visit their hockey-playing friend Sammy Fox on the Tumbling Waters Indian Reservation, they are soon required to show courage and stealth when tested by Chief Saskamoose and members of the tribe. Failure will result in severe punishment that Elmo Swift, a bitter young man, says he would happily apply to the Mitchell brothers personally.

Max and Marty quickly befriend members of the community when they are recruited to play the ancient and exciting game of lacrosse during a pow-wow celebration. Then they spring into action when a group of armed and arrogant miners from the nearby town of Silver Creek—led by the notorious Blackjack Bradley—try to force Sammy and the Tumbling Water residents from their land.

It's another dangerous and thrilling adventure for the Mitchell brothers—when they move, Among the Indians.